—— SPY CLUB BOOK TWO ——

THE VALLEY VILLAGES SUMMER SHOW

BOBBEE MELLOR

Grosvenor House
Publishing Limited

This book is published by
Grosvenor House Publishing Ltd
Link House
140 The Broadway, Tolworth, Surrey, KT6 7HT.
www.grosvenorhousepublishing.co.uk

This book is a work of fiction. Any resemblance to
people or events, past or present, is purely coincidental.

A CIP record for this book
is available from the British Library

ISBN 978-1-80381-253-3

CHAPTER ONE

Life in the Valley Villages was full of excitement and anticipation. The coming weekend was August Bank Holiday and that meant the Valley Villages Summer Show. It was the highlight of the villagers' year and preparations had been going on for months.

Ma and Pa Dawson were busily involved in the preparations, Ma being one of the overall organisers and in charge of the tea tent and Pa overseeing all the show's finances.

Their four Siamese cats, Jake, Libby, Ginny and Wesley, were usually equally excited, as they spent a lot of time at the showground during the week of preparation. Ma and Pa parked their caravan on the edge of the car park, behind the tea tent and, during the day, the cats wandered in and out to their hearts' content and enjoyed the change of scenery. For some reason, over the years, a lot of the villagers had got into the habit of taking their pets to the showground, so there were always a lot of familiar cats and dogs wandering around.

Somehow though, this year, the four cats didn't feel the same kind of excitement as they had in previous years. They had recently experienced something which made the Summer Show seem rather tame. Earlier in the summer the villages had been the victims of a pair of nasty young burglars. Led by Jake, some of the villages' cats and dogs had planned a campaign that led to the capture of the two thieves. It had been an exciting and occasionally dangerous time, and the weeks since had seemed rather flat. Even the prospect of the Summer Show didn't come close to the thrills they had experienced when they had been plotting and planning their operation.

Wesley, the youngest and smallest of Ma and Pa's cats, cheekily referred to them all as Jake's Spy Club, a name Jake secretly rather liked. The club was made up of cats and dogs from across the villages and they had worked out a very efficient system of communication. The animals had continued to keep in touch, always secretly hoping that their skills would be needed again but, after a few days of excitement and talk, the villages had settled back into their usual humdrum routine.

To be honest, Libby and Ginny were quite glad to go back to their usual quiet pace of life; at times things had been more than a little frightening, especially when Ginny's boyfriend, Sherpa, the next-door neighbour's cat, had nearly been seriously hurt during the final ambush.

The Tuesday morning before the show the four cats were lying in their favourite place, under the apple tree at the top of the big garden, enjoying the late summer sun and talking about the Summer Show. Ma was at the showground helping to organise things – the tea tent was being put up and she liked to be there to supervise. Pa had gone to collect the caravan and park it in its usual place. They would all be going to the showground the next day.

"It'll be fun going to the showground again, won't it?" said Wesley, hoping to rouse some interest in Jake.

"Yes, I suppose so," said Jake, not particularly enthusiastically. "It just doesn't seem as exciting and different as it used to."

"Well, at least we'll get to see Brian and Max and some of the others who don't live in Lower Barton." Wesley was determined to be positive.

2

Max was Jake's brother who lived with Ma's sister, known by everyone as Mad Mary, in the next but one village and Brian, a big, brown mongrel, belonged to Ma and Pa's daughter, Claire. Both were members of Jake's Spy Club.

"If Mad Mary's there with Max, she'll have that stupid dog with her as well." Jake was determined not to show any enthusiasm too soon. The other three cats looked slightly horrified when Jake reminded them of Mad Mary's newly acquired pet. A few weeks earlier a stray dog, thin and dirty, had turned up on her smallholding and had promptly been adopted.

"I'd forgotten about Tarran," said Wesley, looking rather glum.

"Who could forget Tarran?" responded Ginny grumpily. "With him it's a case of once met, never forgotten."

Libby smiled at Ginny. "Oh, he's not so bad," she said tolerantly. "He's only young. He'll learn."

Wesley giggled. "If Max has anything to do with it, he'll learn very quickly."

To the amusement of the four cats, Tarran had taken on Max, thinking he would be an easy conquest, only to find himself with a severely scratched nose and his ears soundly boxed. He had been very wary of Max since then. Clearly the big cat was no pushover.

Still trying to be positive Libby said, "Just remember, we didn't always think very much of Brian until he proved us wrong."

It was true that the four cats had tended to be rather unkind to the gentle natured dog, thinking him a wimp. However, he had proved himself to be a good friend and an asset to Spy Club. No-one knew this better than Wesley, whose life Brian had saved when Wesley was attacked by a vicious dog named Bozo. The big dog was now a welcome visitor to the Dawson house, much to his great pleasure.

"I suppose so," said Jake, responding to Libby's comment. "Tarran's just such a pain. He never shuts up and he's always doing something he shouldn't. He'll spoil being at the showground."

"Come on Jake, snap out of it," said Libby, rather sharply. "It's not like you to be so negative."

"Besides which," added Wesley, "he might be a recruit for Jake's Spy Club." Then he rolled over, laughing at the thought of the boisterous dog being any use in a tough situation. The three other cats joined in his laughter.

"Who might be a new recruit?" came a voice from further down the garden, as Sherpa appeared through the gap in the hedge between the two gardens and made his way up the garden to the apple tree. He rubbed his head against Ginny and, with a "Hallo, Girl", sat down beside her.

"Tarran!" snorted Wesley, still overcome with laughter. The other cats, even Jake, started laughing again at the amazed expression on Sherpa's face.

"I hope you're not serious. That dog's a liability." Sherpa had only met Tarran once but, as Ginny had suggested, once was enough.

"Anyway," continued Sherpa, "are you lot off to the showground tomorrow?"

"Yes," said Ginny, "but Jake's being grumpy about it. He wants to be out catching bad guys."

"Be careful what you wish for," laughed Sherpa.

"Yes, okay," replied Jake. "I suppose we can't have thrilling events happening every week. We'll just have to make the most of another enjoyable but uneventful Summer Show." And the others all nodded in agreement.

However, in thinking this Jake was quite wrong. This year's Summer Show was destined to be anything but uneventful!

CHAPTER TWO

Wednesday morning dawned bright and sunny. After a quick breakfast the four cats were put into the back of Pa's four by four and they all drove to the showground. It was a few miles away in two fields between the villages of Avebury and Little Longton, which a local farmer allowed them to use every year. As they drove along even Jake began to feel the familiar sense of anticipation and excitement.

Pa parked the car beside the caravan, already in place behind the tea tent, which had been put up but not yet connected to an electricity supply. The tea tent was always the first to go up, not just to supply tea and coffee for all the volunteers putting the showground together but because it formed a meeting place for people from the different villages to catch up with each other.

The showground was already busy with things being delivered and places being marked out. There was a general air of activity and anticipation, which the cats remembered from previous years. Ma opened the caravan door and clipped it back so that the cats could come and go as they pleased. She knew they wouldn't go far and would be quite safe.

The cats walked into the tea tent where a couple of men were putting up tables and chairs, piles of which were lying on the grass outside the tent. As usual everything was running smoothly; Ma and the rest of her committee were well organised.

To Jake's relief Mad Mary hadn't yet arrived, but Libby noticed Claire on the far side of the field, Brian by her side.

The big dog suddenly caught sight of his friends and lolloped joyfully across the field.

"Hallo you lot," he panted. "Isn't this fun?"

"Yes," said Libby kindly. "It's a lot of fun. What's Claire doing over there? That's where the secretary's tent goes. I thought she did the tombola and helped in the tea tent?"

Brian looked glum. "She's trying to find a copy of the dog show classes to see if there's one she can enter me in."

The four cats struggled not to laugh, not wanting to offend their friend but Brian, not a dog you would connect with dog shows, looked so downcast that eventually they could control themselves no longer. The four of them burst out laughing, the thought of Brian in a dog show was just too funny and eventually Brian joined in.

"I'm not a dog show dog, am I?" he said. The cats shook their heads, but loyal little Wesley spoke up.

"You're much too good for a dog show. If they knew what you can do, they would give you a huge red rosette and a big cup. I bet those dogs in the shows couldn't have sent Bozo on his way with his tail between his legs."

Jake suddenly snorted with laughter again. "Perhaps Mad Mary will enter Tarran."

There was a stunned silence as the five animals tried to picture Tarran let loose in a show ring. The idea was just ridiculous and all of them, even Brian, lay on the floor laughing, imagining the chaos he would cause.

Ma looked across at the rolling animals with a frown. "What's up with them?" she said to Pa. "Are they alright? They all look as if they're in pain. Do you think they've eaten something that's made them ill?"

Pa glanced at them and said, "They're having a stretch. Enjoying the freedom of being here." He sounded as if he was trying to persuade himself rather than persuade Ma. The animals' behaviour during the time of the village burglaries had caused Pa some concern. An intelligent, logical man, he had tried hard to find intelligent, logical explanations for their behaviour. However, in spite of what his common sense told him he had found it very hard.

The animals, having stopped laughing, were just about to go exploring when they heard the clanking and rattling which meant that Mad Mary's old Land Rover had arrived. They waited for Tarran to burst into the tea tent. Then suddenly they heard a shout from halfway across the field.

"For goodness' sake, Mary, put that lunatic dog on a lead before he wrecks everything." Tarran had evidently arrived!

Shortly after, a stately, dark coloured Siamese appeared at the entrance to the tea tent, with a very longsuffering expression on his face.

"I thought I'd find you lot in here. It'll be a relief to have some reasonably intelligent conversation."

"What did he do?" asked Libby, sympathetically.

"Knocked a pile of boxes over, tipping the contents everywhere," replied Max.

At that moment Mad Mary appeared with Tarran on a lead, pulling hard, tongue hanging out. He was good looking for a dog whose breeding was clearly rather mixed and, thanks to

Mad Mary, he was no longer thin and dirty but well fed with a shiny coat. He was totally uncontrolled but, as Libby had said, he was only just out of puppyhood and had obviously never been taught how to behave.

Mad Mary tied Tarran to a solid looking post, near to where Jake and the others were sitting, and went off to speak to Ma. Tarran looked sulky at being tied up and started to complain.

"It's your own fault," said Max, sternly. "You need to behave with more self-control."

Tarran lay down with his head on his paws. He wasn't going to argue with Max – he was indeed a quick learner!

Suddenly the animals could hear a commotion outside. Someone was obviously very angry. They all got up to go outside to investigate, leaving poor Tarran tied up in the tent. When they got outside, they saw a little group of villagers looking both angry and upset.

Ma and Mad Mary came out to find out what was wrong. One of the group, a soldierly looking man, said angrily, "Someone's been and cut up all the ropes for the show rings. Absolutely useless now."

The ropes had been delivered the day before and stored at the side of the field. It hadn't occurred to anyone that they wouldn't be safe there.

"Cut the ropes?" said Mad Mary, incredulously.

Ma looked as shocked as everyone else and then, almost immediately, began to think of the practical problems the damage would cause.

"Will we be able to get more in time, Colonel?" she asked, anxiously. As one of the organisers, she knew how far in advance things had to be booked and how expensive they would be to replace. The Colonel shrugged. They would just have to hope that someone somewhere had ropes to hire out.

"Does the insurance cover us for damage like this?" asked a worried looking woman. Pa looked thoughtful. "We've never had to claim for vandalism before. I'll have to check the policy. It's in the caravan. I'll go and have a look." He strode off into the tea tent and out through the back entrance flap to the caravan.

"Why would anyone do such a horrid thing?" said Mad Mary. "Everyone loves the show. Why would anyone want to spoil it?"

Jake nodded at the other animals and started to walk away from the group of angry humans. They all followed him back inside the tea tent.

"Why would anyone want to do something like that?" asked Libby.

Tarran got up, pulling at his lead. "Do what? What's happened?"

Max looked briefly at him. "Lie down and be quiet, Tarran." Tarran immediately lay down, looking sulky. Libby took pity on him.

"Some horrible person has cut up all the ropes they use for the show rings."

"Well?" said Jake. "What are we going to do about it?" There was a silence. Jake went on, "And before anyone says `what can we do we're just cats` remember last time."

Libby sighed. "Oh Jake, forget last time. You're determined to find something to investigate, but really what can we do? I bet even the humans would have problems finding out who did this. It's a one-off bit of vandalism. Probably some teenagers, immature enough to think it was funny."

"Nobody from the villages would do something like that," said Wesley. "Not even teenagers. Even the people from Littlebury love the show."

"Every town has some people who are less than nice," said Ginny, wisely. "But I agree with you Wesley. Even the Littlebury biker gang come to the show and never cause any trouble."

Wesley grinned. "You're right. Last year I saw one of them walking round with a big fluffy toy. He must have won it on one of the stalls, but he looked really odd carrying it around, dressed in all his biker gear. His mates were taking the mickey out of him all afternoon."

The others smiled at the picture Wesley had conjured up, but nobody said anything.

At that moment Ma, Mad Mary and Claire appeared at the opening to the tea tent, all looking, like the other villagers, both upset and angry. Ma turned to the other two. "Grab some cups and saucers, will you? There's milk and sugar in the blue cool bag. We're not going to be connected to an electricity supply until this afternoon, but I'll put the kettle on in the caravan. I think everyone could do with a nice cup of tea after such a nasty shock."

She went through the flap at the back of the tent, while Claire and Mad Mary started laying out cups and saucers and getting milk and sugar from one of several cool bags Ma had brought with her.

The animals watched in silence. It was not a nice way to start the week. Claire went off to tell all the helpers that tea and coffee would be provided in the tea tent before everyone prepared for some hard work.

The animals all settled down to keep the humans company while they had their drinks and, truthfully, to eavesdrop on their conversation in case there was anything useful to be learned. Jake, especially, listened carefully. He couldn't quite rid himself of the wish to take a hand in solving the question of who had cut the ropes.

The volunteers were all grateful for the drinks and cheered up considerably. It was a setback, they felt, but that was all. Pa had discovered that the insurance did cover them for vandalism and the Colonel, having spent some time on his mobile talking to various contacts who might be able to help, had miraculously found a company able to provide them with more ropes, which would arrive on Thursday. The news cheered everyone up and, now the shock of what had happened had worn off, people found their enthusiasm rising again and they went back to their tasks with renewed energy.

CHAPTER THREE

The rest of the day passed uneventfully. The humans busied themselves getting the showground up and running, determined to show the unkind vandal that they had not succeeded in spoiling the show.

Two policemen had come to the showground, following Pa's reporting of the vandalism but, after looking at the ropes and shaking their heads in disgust, they admitted there was little they could do. They took a statement from the Colonel and one of the policemen, PC Watkins, took pictures of the ropes and promised to log the incident. However, as they left the showground, it was clear that they didn't hold out much hope of catching the culprit.

The animals spent the time alternately sitting in the tea tent and wandering freely around the showground, watching the progress of the work, checking out the newly erected tents and stalls and socialising with any animals with whom they happened to be acquainted. Tarran was left tied up in the tent, so they were spared any annoyance from him, but kind Libby made sure they returned regularly to give him some company.

The first time they went back to see him he wasn't a bit grateful and complained about being left tied up on his own while they all went off enjoying themselves. Even Libby was rather taken aback at his behaviour. However, Max had told him very forcefully that he only had himself to blame and, if he didn't show a little more gratitude, they would leave him there alone all day every day.

Knowing that Max was quite capable of doing just that, Tarran was far more pleasant on their next visit and Max, realising that he had made his point, said no more about abandoning him. Jake and the others were amused at how easily Max dominated a dog who was at least twice, if not three times, his size.

At lunch time most of the workers gathered in the tea tent to eat the packed lunches they had brought with them, the food vans not yet being on site. Ma once again made tea for everyone with the caravan kettle. Later in the day the electricity was connected, and Ma was able to produce a steady flow of tea and coffee using the big tea urn, for which the hardworking villagers were very thankful. Much as they all enjoyed preparing for the show, it was hard, thirsty work.

The villagers spent most of lunchtime discussing the damaged ropes and trying to work out who could have done such a thing but, like the cats and Brian, they could think of no-one who would be that spiteful. The best anyone could manage was 'thugs from the town on a drunken spree'!

Jake was not impressed. "We thought of that. You'd think humans would have more ideas."

"Humans are really quite unimaginative," said Max sarcastically.

They were interrupted by Mad Mary coming to take Tarran for a walk. She was a doting owner to her animals, but even she would not risk the wrath of the villagers by setting Tarran loose. She already loved him dearly, but she knew as well as everybody else that the unruly dog could not be trusted to behave and would cause chaos wherever he went.

In the afternoon, as the animals were having another wander around the showground, they came across a rather scruffy black and white cat, well known to them.

"Hallo, Mangy Tom, what are you doing here?" asked Libby, surprised to see him. Tom had never been known to visit the showground. He was a stray who wandered the villages, sleeping wherever he felt like and with regular feeding places amongst the villagers. He was an independent cat, but he had been an invaluable asset to Spy Club and had become their messenger, going from village to village passing on information and instructions. He had also provided Jake, Ginny and Wesley with a great deal of amusement by taking a fancy to Libby and telling her that she was 'a fine-looking cat'!

"Didn't have anything particular to do," he said casually, "so thought I'd pop over and see what all the fuss was about. I knew you lot would be here. How are you doing, Beautiful?" he added looking at Libby, who would have blushed if cats could blush, but she simply smiled and shook her head at the stray's impudence and then looked hard at Wesley, who was grinning and about to say something cheeky.

When he heard about the damaged ropes, Tom was surprised but not particularly concerned. He tended to be a carefree cat not particularly attached to anyone or anything. His friendship with Jake and the others was the first he had ever had and, to his surprise, he rather liked it.

"Well, what are you going to do about it?" he asked the others.

"Nothing!" said Libby firmly. "There's nothing we can do. It's probably a group of kids being silly." She was determined not to encourage Jake to start imagining there was anything they could do.

Mangy Tom was happy to chat with them but didn't stay long. He left when the others decided to return to the tea tent, promising to call back again the next day.

Later in the afternoon Sally, the vicar, dropped by and brought her cat, Beelzebub, with her. He, too, was a member of Spy Club and joined Jake and the other animals who were still in the tea tent visiting Tarran.

Beelzebub had already heard about the vandalism. As the local vicar Sally heard all the news and, therefore, so did Beelzebub. Unlike Mangy Tom, he was very angry about the damaged ropes, partly because the news of the spiteful act had upset Sally. She was very proud of the way the members of the different villages worked together to make the show a success each year.

While the vicar went over to Ma and the others to have a cup of tea and hear all the details of the vandalism, Beelzebub settled with Jake and the other animals. Tarran hadn't met the big black cat before and got a little over excited. Before he had a chance to do anything too silly, Wesley said jokingly, "Watch your nose, Tarran. Beelzebub has a powerful set of claws and he's not afraid to use them." The others laughed as Tarran sat back and looked rather cautious, especially when Beelzebub raised a front paw and extended a set of lethal looking claws.

"Okay, I get the message," said Tarran, rather crossly, and lay down with his head on his paws feeling hard done by and rather left out of things. He would have loved to go over and join the other animals and be part of their friendship group, but he knew he wasn't wanted and he knew it was his own fault. He just didn't know what to do about it.

The vicar stayed chatting with Ma and the others for a few minutes and then went to look at the work going on around the showground, taking her cat with her. When they had left Mad Mary took Tarran for a walk again, leaving the five cats and Brian to wander outside and settle down to sleep in the sun.

When Wesley woke up, he noticed that Brian was also awake, although the others slept on. Since their adventure together with Bozo the two had become firm friends. Wesley looked at Brian and said quietly, so as not to wake the others, "Shall we go and look at the cut ropes?" Brian nodded. He, too, was curious as to what exactly had been done to them.

The two friends strolled across the field towards the area where they knew the ropes were always stored. When they got there, they stood looking in silence at the pile of damaged ropes. The ropes had been hacked quite savagely apart. Wesley and Brian looked at each other. A shiver went down Wesley's back. "I don't like the look of them at all," he said. "That doesn't look to me like mindless vandalism. That was meant."

Brian nodded. "Shall we tell Jake and the others?" Wesley thought for a minute. "I don't think there's any point. We can't do anything and it'll only get Jake worked up again, and that will annoy Libby. Best keep it to ourselves." Brian nodded again. "Okay. I think you're right. But it's not nice, is it?"

Which, in Wesley's mind, was something of an understatement.

They wandered back to the tea tent where they found the other animals awake and wondering what had happened to Brian and Wesley.

"Where have you two been?" asked Jake.

"You lot were still snoring when we woke up, so we went for a walk round the showground. It's coming on well." said Wesley, casually. The others seemed to accept what he said without question, but he felt a bit uncomfortable when he caught Libby looking at him thoughtfully. She said nothing, though, and he was able to relax.

The workers were beginning to slow down and were getting ready to pack up for the day. Some came into the tea tent for a final cup of tea and the cats wandered outside to watch the clearing up. Before he knew what was happening Wesley found himself a little apart from the others with a determined Libby by his side.

"Okay," she said. "What did you and Brian see?"

Wesley looked at her, debating whether to make something up, but he knew that wise Libby would see right through him. He told her the truth. She looked very serious as she listened but said, "You were right to keep quiet about it. It would only get Jake worked up for no reason. You're a sensible little thing, aren't you?" She nodded approvingly at him and went to join the others. For some reason Wesley felt a great deal better for having told Libby.

By the end of the day, the helpers had all done a lot of hard work and everyone went home satisfied with the progress achieved in spite of the unhappy start to the day. By the time everybody was ready to leave the showground both humans and animals were tired and glad to get back to their homes, eat a good meal and settle down to sleep.

However, three of the animals were not as relaxed as they pretended to be and Libby and Wesley especially, were unsettled by the thought of the spite that had gone into the cutting of the ropes. They said nothing to Jake and Ginny but couldn't help wondering if there was more to come.

CHAPTER FOUR

At half past six on Thursday morning the cats were disturbed by the ringing of the telephone. Ma and Pa, already up and getting ready for another busy day, appeared in the kitchen and Ma went over and answered the phone. The cats could hear agitated squawking on the other end of the phone and Ma's face drained of colour.

"What?" she gasped. Pa went over to her and she passed the phone to him, then collapsed into a chair looking absolutely shocked. Pa gave her a quick concerned look and then turned to the phone.

"Hello, who is it?" asked Pa. The squawking came again and Pa, not wasting time on talk, said briefly, "We'll be there shortly," and put the phone down.

The cats, unable to understand what the squawking voice had said, could only assume that something else had happened at the showground. They were proved right with Ma's next words.

"Who could be doing this, Pa? Why are they trying to spoil the show?"

"I don't know, love," said Pa. "Come on, we better get over there." He disappeared out of the kitchen to continue getting ready.

"I'd better feed the cats first," said Ma, and quickly put down four bowls of food. Then she followed Pa out of the kitchen.

"Come on, we better eat." said Jake. "It sounds like we're going to need our strength today. I wonder what's happened now. It sounds bad."

The cats quickly cleared their dishes and went to wait by the back door. They didn't want to risk being left behind. They were worried that whatever had happened would make Ma think it was safer to leave them at home.

Ma and Pa came back to the kitchen, collected the boxes of things they had put ready the night before, and then they all went out to Pa's car. It was clear that Ma intended to have the cats safely with her and Pa.

As they were getting into the car, they saw Sherpa sitting on the wall of his front garden. Jake called out, "Something's happened at the showground. Can you get there?"

Sherpa stood up and stretched. "I'll be there. What's up now?" He had heard about the damaged ropes from Beelzebub the night before.

"Don't know," replied Jake, "but it sounds serious. See you there."

During the journey to the showground Ma phoned Mad Mary to tell her all about it and the cats found out exactly what had happened.

"Mary, someone's poured paint over the stalls that were put up yesterday. I know ... yes ... I know. Dreadful. Okay we'll see you there."

The cats looked at each other. What on earth was going on?

It didn't take long to get to the showground, where they were met by an extremely angry Colonel, the person who had phoned Ma and Pa, and two other members of the committee, a middle-aged man called Geoff and a young woman, who was the show secretary, Jenny. The three of them were clearly glad to see Ma and Pa.

After Ma and Pa had had a brief word with the Colonel, they all went over to where the stalls were being put up. Fortunately, only four of the stalls had gone up the previous day, but those four were completely covered in splashes of red paint. Everyone gazed in horror at the mess in front of them.

"What are we going to do?" said Ma, despairingly.

"Well, for a start, I've phoned and reported it to the police," said the Colonel. "They've said they'll send someone out but, no doubt, they'll say there's nothing to be done again." He looked a little impatient as he said this. He was a man who felt there was always something that could be done. He continued,

"I've also phoned the owner of the company which rents them to us and he's coming out. He should be here soon. What on earth we're going to say to him I can't imagine! He's got every right to be absolutely furious. I don't suppose there's any way to clean them up completely and it'll take ages."

"Well, there's nothing we can do until he gets here," said Pa as calmly as he could. "Come over to the tea tent. We could all do with a reviving drink."

Glad of something to do Ma, closely followed by the cats, rushed ahead to get the urn filled and switched on. Once they were all provided with a hot drink, the humans settled themselves at one of the tables and the cats stayed close by so that they could listen in to the conversation. The Colonel echoed what everyone was thinking. "Who's doing this? What have they got against the village show?"

But no-one had an answer. They were all baffled.

They were in the process of drinking their tea when the Colonel's mobile rang. The owner of the stalls had arrived at the showground. Feeling rather nervous at facing the person whose property had been damaged while it was in their possession, everyone left their drinks and, followed as usual by the cats, went to meet the owner, who was standing staring at his damaged stalls.

"It's a bit of a mess, isn't it?" he said to them.

"Yes," said the Colonel, feeling rather embarrassed, as if he was personally responsible for allowing the man's property to end up in this state. "I'm really sorry. We have no idea who is doing all this damage."

The man, whose name was Mr. Browning, raised his eyebrows. "Yes, I heard about the damaged ropes. Sounds nasty."

"Someone seems to have something against the show and is trying to cause trouble, but we just can't think who or why." said Pa. "Fortunately we are covered for vandalism, so we'll be able to pay to replace the stalls."

Mr Browning smiled, to the great relief of the other humans. He was clearly not angry, as they had expected him to be. "We'll talk about that later. We need to think what you're going to do about these. I assume you need all ten of the stalls you ordered?"

Everyone nodded. "I don't have any more available at the moment," continued Mr Browning, looking thoughtful.

"Well, we'll just have to put up some tables or something," said Pa.

"Why don't you finish what the vandals started?" suggested Mr Browning. Everyone looked at him in confusion.

"What do you mean?" asked Pa, privately wondering if Mr. Browning was a little unhinged!

"Paint the stalls in a variety of bright colours," responded Mr Browning. "Would you have time to do that?"

"You wouldn't mind us doing that?" said Ma.

Mr Browning smiled. "Not at all. My wife was born and bred in these villages. If I didn't try to help the show, she'd never speak to me again."

"Have we time?" asked Jenny, the show secretary.

The Colonel, thankful that Mr. Browning was being so helpful and glad to have something positive to do, put his shoulders back and said firmly, "We'll make time. I'll get on the phone and get some extra volunteers. And we'll need to go out and get some paint."

"I'll provide that," said Mr Browning. "I've got a contact in the paint business owes me a favour or two. I'll be back soon." And he strode off towards his car.

"What a nice man!" said Ma, watching him go with a smile on her face. "He restores your faith in people." Then she turned to the others and said, briskly, "Well come on you lot, let's get sorted. No time to waste."

However, before they could make a move to return to the tea tent, they saw a police car turn into the showground entrance and park on the edge of the field. PC Watkins and the other policeman from the day before got out of the car and wandered over to the group standing by the damaged stalls. They both looked in silence at the paint splattered stalls and shook their heads.

PC Watkins said, sympathetically, "Someone's obviously got it in for your show. Any idea who it might be?" The humans all shook their heads.

Again, the policeman took some photos of the vandalised stalls and a statement from the Colonel, but once more he shook his head regretfully, indicating that there was little chance of any success in finding out who was responsible.

"I'm really sorry," PC Watkins said. "My sister is married to a village man and they live in Great Longton. I know how much this show means to you all. I really wish we could give you a more positive response."

Pa nodded and said, "Well thanks for coming out anyway." He shook the policeman's hand and then the two policemen made their way back to their car and drove off in the direction of Littlebury.

The Colonel and Pa shrugged as they watched them leave. They were not really surprised at what the police had said. They knew that the local police force was only small and had other more serious crimes to investigate. Ma said, "Well we've just got to press on and do the best we can," and she went off to put the tea urn on – her cure for all ills.

CHAPTER FIVE

The animals were not particularly impressed by the lack of encouragement from the police and Jake secretly felt that Spy Club needed to get involved in the situation. He'd have to work on Libby!

"It doesn't look like any of the humans are going to do anything helpful," he said, looking at the others hopefully.

Libby tried to be fair to the policemen who had come out. "He was nice, the policeman," she said. "He obviously felt sorry that they couldn't help."

The others nodded and then, feeling that nothing more was to be learnt by staying near the stalls, they made their way back to the tea tent and settled in their usual place. Jake looked at all the others but said nothing. Then he looked meaningfully at Libby, although he still said nothing. Finally, Libby said, "Okay, okay. I give in. I agree. There's something going on which needs looking into."

The others, glad that a decision seemed to have been made, all nodded. Wesley said, "Someone's trying to spoil the show but why?"

"If we knew that we'd have some idea who's doing this," replied Jake.

Before they could continue their discussion, they heard the unmistakeable rattle of Mad Mary's Land Rover and, seconds later, Max appeared in the tea tent looking very serious.

He nodded at the others and then said, "Well Jake, it looks like your Spy Club is needed again."

All four cats nodded. Max's comment seemed to seal the decision. If Max thought the animals should get involved, they knew that they were right.

"We were just saying that," said Libby. "Something horrible is going on. Someone is trying to spoil the show. We just can't think why."

At that moment Ma came into the tent with Mad Mary, who had Tarran on his lead. She tied him to his usual post and went over to the tea urn with Ma. They were expecting to be making vast quantities of tea over the next few hours, to keep all the volunteer painters going!

The cats nodded at Tarran, who pulled at his lead trying to get free.

"Stop it, Tarran." said Max quietly and Tarran lay down, looking resentfully at the cats.

"What are we going to do, Jake?" asked Wesley, wondering what they actually *could* do.

Jake looked round and said decisively, "We're going to have to get some of the team to patrol the showground at night. At least if anyone does anything else, we'll have some idea of who it is."

"How many have we got who can be out at night?" asked Ginny. "Sherpa can."

"Beelzebub, Leo and Mangy Tom," added Libby.

"Maybe Sooty and Patch will help," suggested Wesley.

The two cats lived in Garston with a Retriever called Jasper, Brian's good friend, and were Spy Club members.

Before anyone had a chance to say any more the vicar walked into the tea tent, closely followed by Beelzebub and, to everyone's amazement, a grinning Sherpa.

"Sherps!" said Ginny, joyfully. "How did you get here so quickly?"

"Cadged a lift from the vicar," Sherpa replied cheerfully, as if it was quite a natural thing for a cat to do.

The other cats looked at him in amazement and then Libby said, "How on earth did you manage to do that?"

"I'd been talking to Beelzebub and as he got into her car so did I. You know the vicar. She waited a couple of seconds to see if I'd get out, then just shrugged and shut the door."

"Have you heard about the paint?" asked Jake. The two cats nodded.

"Someone phoned Sally," said Beelzebub. "That's why we've come over. She's really mad about it." It was obvious that Beelzebub was pretty mad about it himself. Whatever upset Sally, upset him. "Have they managed to sort anything out?" he continued.

Jake explained about Mr Browning's suggestion and then went on, "We've just said we need to get whoever we can to patrol the ground at night. There's not much we can do, I'm afraid." He nodded at Libby, Ginny and Wesley. "Ma's a stickler for checking we're in at night."

Both Sherpa and Beelzebub said they would be able to help and Beelzebub felt sure Leo would too. He and the ginger cat were great friends and he had already told Leo about the cut ropes.

The animals were just considering how they were going to arrange the nightly patrols, when Pa came into the tent and had a low conversation with Ma. Ma kept nodding her head and the animals were longing to hear what they were saying. Eventually Pa left the tent and Ma turned to Mad Mary and Sally and said, "Pa thinks we should stay overnight to keep an eye on things."

Ma's cats pricked up their ears. "That sounds like a good idea," Mad Mary was saying. "Will you keep the cats with you?"

"Oh yes," replied Ma. "The caravan is plenty big enough. They'll be wandering around the showground all day, so they'll probably just sleep all night. Pa and I can pop home if ever we need to get anything."

Jake and the others looked at each other gleefully. If Ma and Pa were going to stay at the showground overnight, then Jake and the other three would at least be on site if anything happened.

Before they had a chance to discuss this new development, Claire and Brian appeared at the entrance, Claire looking both angry and concerned. Brian went over to the group of animals, who all nodded a welcome but were too busy listening intently to the humans' conversation to do more.

"Oh Ma," said Claire, despairingly. "What on earth is going on?"

Ma shook her head. "I really don't know love. Pa and I have decided that we're going to stay overnight in the caravan until the show is over, keep an eye on things. Pa will go round the showground a couple of times throughout the night to check on everything."

Claire nodded. "That sounds like a good idea. But be careful. We don't know what sort of person or people we're dealing with."

Libby looked very thoughtful when she heard Claire say that. Claire continued, "Why don't you keep Brian with you? I know he's a soft old thing but, if you do come across the vandals, the sight of a big dog might make them back off."

Mary nodded as Ma appeared to be thinking over what Claire had suggested. The cats waited anxiously hoping that she would accept Claire's offer. They knew better than anyone that the 'soft old thing' was a demon when roused. It would be brilliant to have him there if anything did happen. Ma eventually nodded. "I'll have a word with Pa, but I think you're probably right, if you don't mind leaving him here."

Claire laughed. "He loves being with your cats these days. It's funny how they suddenly all became friends. They used to be quite standoffish with him."

The cats looked at Brian guiltily, but he smiled back. "I'm glad we're friends now."

"It'll be great if you're going to be here with us overnight," said Libby.

Ginny groaned. "But we'll still be shut in. I wish Ma didn't worry about us so much."

"We'll deal with that when the time comes." said Jake. "We sorted it last time and we'll do it again if necessary." He couldn't help feeling satisfied with the way things were going. Now, if anything did occur at night, most of the Spy Club members would be there to deal with it, one way or another.

At that moment Pa came into the tea tent with the Colonel and two other men. "Mr Browning has brought a load of paint back and we've several people offering to come and paint the stalls as they go up." said the Colonel. "We're starting now with the four that have been vandalised." Ma handed him a cup of tea and he nodded his thanks and then continued, "Pa has told me that you plan to stay in your caravan until the show's over. Very good of you. Think it's a good idea but be careful. Whoever's doing this could be dangerous."

Ma told them about Claire's offer to leave Brian with them and Pa nodded his agreement. He couldn't help looking at the group of animals who, to him, seemed to be listening intently to the conversation. He could swear that they had extremely satisfied looks on their faces when it was agreed to have Brian there. He turned away and thought to himself, 'You're losing it, old man. Get a grip!'

He turned back to Ma and clapped his hands. "Come on ladies, where's the tea? We hardworking men need refreshment."

Ma smiled. "If you're not careful, we'll leave you to make it yourselves." But she went back to the urn and started sorting out the tea.

Once the humans were busy with their cups of tea, Libby turned to look at Wesley and Brian. "I think now we ought to tell the others what you saw yesterday. This is obviously more serious than we thought."

The other cats looked questioningly at Brian and the other two. "What are you on about?" asked Jake. Libby nodded at Wesley. "Go on."

Wesley took a deep breath and then started to tell the interested cats about his walk with Brian and what they had felt when they saw the damaged ropes. Jake and Ginny listened wide eyed, asking questions every now and then, but Max sat quietly, looking very serious.

"Why didn't you tell us yesterday?" asked Jake, not very pleased to have been left out. Wesley looked guilty but Libby came to his rescue. "It didn't seem worth it. We all thought the damage to the ropes was a one off. Now we know it wasn't."

Jake looked at the three of them and then nodded. "It seems to me that this person, or these people, have a nasty streak and we need to be watching out. We'd better warn the others not to take any chances when they're patrolling."

The animals sat silently for a minute, remembering the dangers they had faced in their last investigation. It was clear that they were going to have to be very, very careful.

CHAPTER SIX

Having drunk her tea, the vicar decided to go and have a look at the damaged stalls before they were painted over, and Claire went with her. Pa and the others were getting ready to go back to work when it occurred to Ma that they had none of them had any breakfast. Once they had electricity in the tent, Ma had set up a two-ring hot plate. She now proceeded to get rolls and bacon out of one of the many cool bags she had brought with her. She turned to Mad Mary and said, "Can you get some bacon on? We'll provide breakfast for everyone before they get started." She shouted across to Pa on his way out of the tent," Pa, can you tell everyone – hot drinks and bacon rolls in ten minutes?"

Pa went off and the Colonel and the other two men sat down again, looking enthusiastic. "Jolly good of you, Ma," said the Colonel and the other two nodded.

"You'll be needing it before the day's out," laughed Ma. "There's a great deal of work to be done."

A few minutes later Pa returned, followed by several men and women, all looking eagerly at the bacon sizzling in two large frying pans. They settled themselves at tables next to the Colonel's and were soon tucking in. Brian, with an apologetic look at the cats, went over to sit by the tables. He was rather fond of bacon and, sure enough, several people gave him bits to eat. Mad Mary was generous with the filling of the rolls and there was plenty to spare.

"What about me?" complained Tarran and Mad Mary, hearing him whining, took across some bits of bacon, which disappeared in double quick time. Ma, not wanting the cats to feel left out, took over some cat biscuits for them to share - a treat for Jake and the other three as Ma was sparing with them at home.

After the early morning shock, having tucked into a good breakfast, everyone seemed to have recovered their spirits and went off full of enthusiasm for the tasks ahead. Thanks to Mr Browning's generosity another problem had been dealt with. However, everyone, animal and human, was wondering what would happen next.

Jake looked at the other animals and said, "Shall we go and see if the ropes are still here. I'd like to see them for myself." The others all agreed and Wesley and Brian led the way out of the tent and over to the side of the field, where the ropes were still lying in a heap. The animals stood and looked at them and everyone understood Wesley's comment that it was 'meant'.

"Nasty!" said Max. "They've been slashed with a very sharp knife or something similar. You don't carry something like that on the off chance that you might need it. It was brought deliberately with the intention of doing serious damage."

"Yes." replied Jake. "You're right. We really do need to be careful. Very careful." They were all remembering the frightening moment in July when the young thug had pulled out a knife and threatened Brian.

Jake looked for another minute at the ropes and then turned determinedly away from them and added briskly, "Come on you lot. Let's go and see how they're getting on with the stalls."

When they got to the area where the stalls had been put up, work had already started and Mr. Browning himself was painting enthusiastically. The animals sat down to watch for a while and Libby said, "Thank goodness there are people like Mr Browning as well as nasty vandals."

"Albert," said Wesley, knowingly. The others looked at him with puzzled expressions. "I heard him tell the other helpers to call him Albert."

"Nice name," said Ginny, and they all laughed. Libby looked disapprovingly at them all.

"I don't care what his name is. He's a nice man and we owe him." The others looked rather shamefaced and nodded. She was right. Mr Browning could have been very difficult about the damage. Instead, he had cheerfully solved the problem for them.

Libby went across to the busily painting man and rubbed round his legs, the only way she could think of to thank him for his generosity. He stopped painting and looked down to see who was there.

"Hallo, there. Aren't you a little beauty?" He bent down to give her a stroke and Libby rubbed her head around his hand. One of the other painters looked across and smiled.

"That's one of Ma and Pa's cats," he said. "The others are there as well, along with Mad Mary's cat and Claire's dog. Sometimes there are others trailing round with them. In fact, for a start off I can see the vicar's cat there as well. It gets more like Noah's Ark here every day. Never cause any trouble though."

Feeling she had done her bit for good relations Libby moved away along the row of stalls, followed slowly by the others.

Wesley watched her as she wandered on and then crept up to Jake and whispered wickedly in his ear, "Which one of us is going to tell Libby that she's got streaks of bright yellow paint all over her head?"

Jake looked across at Libby and then back to Wesley. Max, too, heard what Wesley had said and they both frowned at him. Then Jake looked at Libby and, much against his will, a small smile twitched around his mouth.

Soon Ginny and Brian realised what was amusing Wesley. Brian looked at Wesley, then at Libby and then back to Wesley. He gently shook his head and Wesley immediately stopped grinning. When Jake and Max looked at him disapprovingly, he was not much bothered, but when his friend Brian did it, it was a different matter. He went across to Libby and whispered, "Libs, he's left some paint on your head. Do you want me to lick it off?"

Libby smiled affectionately at him. "No thank you Wesley. I'll let you all enjoy the sight of it a bit longer."

If cats could blush Wesley would have looked like a cat shaped tomato. He might have known there was no way you'd get one over on Libby. She was far too smart. The others all smiled at the way Libby had turned the tables on the cheeky little cat, then, fun over, they all returned to watching the painters at work.

After ten minutes they got bored with watching people painting and left to wander round the rest of the showground. When they saw a big van pull up at the far end of the showground, they went over to watch as people started unloading the promised replacement ropes. The van had the name of a town they hadn't heard of on its side, obviously not a local company. The Colonel went over to speak to the driver of the van.

"Hallo John. Thanks so much for this. We're really grateful."

The man called John shook the Colonel's hand. "On the house mate. Can't have anyone spoiling our show."

"It was a way for you to come, though," added the Colonel. "Must be all of seventy miles."

"Well, it'll give me a chance to call in and see Mum and Dad before I go back."

The animals looked at each other. Obviously a local boy. It was good how the village people stuck together, even when they had moved away.

John continued, "I'll be coming to the show on Monday so I can stay on and help take the ropes down. Then I can take them back with me, save two journeys."

The Colonel nodded and the two men joined the others unloading the ropes from the back of the van.

By now it was getting hot and the animals went back to the tea tent to sit in the shade. Mad Mary and Tarran were missing and they presumed she had taken the dog for a walk, but the vicar was in the tent, talking to Ma and Claire. She looked up as the crowd of animals appeared at the entrance. She nodded at Beelzebub and said, "I'm going home now. Are you coming?"

Beelzebub looked at Jake. "I might as well. I'll be back later tonight." He got up and wandered over to Sally, who bent down to stroke him.

Sherpa also got up. "Me too. See you later." He went over to stand by Beelzebub. Sally grinned good naturedly.

"What am I now? The local cat taxi?" She turned to Ma and Claire. "He hitched a lift with me this morning and obviously wants to do the return journey. Come on then, you two." She left the tent followed by the two cats.

Jake and the others had just settled down for a nap when Mad Mary appeared at the entrance with Tarran on his lead, for once not pulling to get away. Mad Mary started to tie him to his post, then looked at him sitting quietly, a little away from the other animals. Feeling sorry for him and thinking he would be too tired from his walk to make a nuisance of himself, she untied him and said, "Behave yourself now or I'll have to tie you up again."

Unable to believe his luck, Tarran moved a bit closer to the others. "Hallo you lot," he said quite quietly. "Where've you been?"

"We've been looking round the showground," said Max. "Where've you been?"

Tarran groaned. "For a long walk. It felt like miles and miles. Mad Mary is a very energetic woman." He promptly put his head on his paws and fell asleep.

Jake sat by Libby and gently licked her head clean. She smiled her thanks and said, "I'll be careful whom I make up to in future and check they've got clean hands. It doesn't do to give that cheeky monkey something to laugh at."

But she looked affectionately at the 'cheeky monkey', who saw her smiling at him and smiled back. Good old Libby. She didn't hold a grudge.

The others were dozing quietly, the heat of the day making them all feel sleepy, but neither Jake nor Libby felt like sleeping. Thoughts of what the night might bring kept them from drifting off and, eventually, they started to talk about the arrangements for patrolling the showground at night.

Jake said, "I wish we could do more, but Ma will never let us out in the dark and I wouldn't want to upset her by running off."

The others, not fully asleep, woke up and joined in the conversation.

"Day or night, take care all of you," said Max. "I'm glad Brian's going to be with you overnight and going on patrol with Pa. A big dog is likely to discourage most people."

Wesley suddenly grinned. "Unless they're called Tarran." Before the others could react, a hurt voice said, "I heard that."

They all looked at Tarran, who had woken up and was listening to the conversation. Max looked severely at the young dog but said, quite tolerantly, "One day you might be a useful dog to have in a tight spot, but not until you learn to behave sensibly."

Tarran lay down and put his head on his paws. Brian, who remembered the time when the cats wanted nothing to do with him either, went over to him and said kindly, "I'm sure Mad Mary will teach you how to behave properly. Just make sure you listen to what she says."

Tarran looked up at the big dog and gave a weak smile. "Okay."

Brian went back to join the others and Jake said, "You big softie." But they all smiled affectionately at the kind natured dog.

CHAPTER SEVEN

At lunchtime the workers all returned to the tea tent to eat their packed lunches and drink the endless cups of tea that Ma, Mad Mary and Claire were providing. Mr Browning came too but had obviously not brought a packed lunch with him, so Ma made him some bacon rolls. He was very hungry after his morning's work and very grateful to Ma for the rolls. She brushed aside his thanks and said, "After what you've done for us, it's a small thing to do. It's we who are grateful to you."

The animals stayed in the tea tent until the workers left, hoping to pick up any interesting information. However, the topic of the vandalism seemed to have been exhausted during the morning and the talk at the lunch tables was to do with the last-minute organisation of the show and, in some cases, who had got through on the latest television talent show!

After lunch the animals, including Tarran, who managed to slip out with them while Mad Mary's back was turned, went outside to have a look around again and were amazed at how much progress had been achieved. Whatever the intention of the vandal the villagers were determined to make sure that the show was going to be the success it always had been.

Six stalls were now up and had been painted in bright colours, which made them look so attractive many people wondered why it hadn't been thought of before. The dog show rings were roped off and most of the competition tents and craft tents were up, with people busy setting up inside them. The secretary's tent had been put up and Jenny was busy laying out everything she would need. They saw Claire going in to speak to her, coming out shortly after with a programme in her hand. Convinced it was to do with the dog show, Brian immediately looked so glum that the cats couldn't help smiling.

For once it was Tarran who said the right thing. "Don't worry, Brian. It could be worse. It could be Mad Mary in there getting a programme."

Max looked at Tarran in surprise. "Nicely said. You're becoming almost human."

Tarran looked at him blankly and even Max realised what a daft thing he'd said. The animals, including Brian, all collapsed with laughter, causing the workers near them to look at the apparently writhing animals with concern.

The little group returned to the tea tent in high spirits, causing Pa, drinking tea with Ma and the others, to look at them rather suspiciously. Mad Mary, concerned that she hadn't seen him slip out of the tent, decided not to take any risks and tied Tarran to his post again, much to his displeasure.

Late in the afternoon, Mad Mary left and took Max and Tarran with her. Max had already told the others they would be leaving early as Mad Mary had some chickens being delivered. Max was not thrilled at the prospect. "We already have a couple of dozen and Mad Mary gives away more eggs than she eats."

To his great pleasure, for once Tarran had been able to go one better than Max.

"Their owner's died." he said. "I heard Mad Mary on the telephone. No-one else wanted them, so she's adopting them like she did me. She's a kind lady."

The cats and Brian had looked at Tarran in astonishment, especially Max, who said, "I think there's hope for you yet."

Then Tarran was the one to look surprised. He had no idea what he'd said to make Max think that, but it made a pleasant change to be complimented for once and not criticised! And when it came time for them to leave Max made no more comments about not needing any more chickens.

When the workers, tired but well satisfied with their efforts, started packing up, Ma tidied up the tea tent and then went to the caravan to make the evening meal for her and Pa. During the afternoon Pa had gone home to collect things they might need and to do some food shopping.

Claire said a fond farewell to Brian and went home to make her husband's tea. Simon usually came to help in the run up to the show, but his company had recently sent him to Dubai for a month to work on a new project and, since he had come back, he had been busy with the final details. However, he had made sure that he had Monday free so that he could come with Claire to the last day of the show.

Eventually everyone except Ma, Pa and the animals had gone. After they had all, animals and humans, had their tea, Ma and Pa took deckchairs to sit outside the tea tent and make the most of the last of the sun. As it started to get dark, they wandered round the showground, along with Brian and the four cats, checking that all was well. Pa was planning to set his alarm for midnight and three in the morning and do more checks with Brian for company. However, Jake and the others knew that, by then, Sherpa, Beelzebub and any other available members of Spy Club would already be on patrol, keeping an all-night vigil and going home when it started to get light.

Once Ma and Pa had gone to their bedroom, the animals made themselves comfortable in the living area, Brian on the rug and the cats on the backs of the settees, where they could see out of the windows. They would be able to watch for any Spy Club members coming to report.

Not long after they had settled down Jake was woken by a quiet "Hi, there", and looked out to see Sherpa and Mangy Tom outside. Sherpa told him that Beelzebub and Leo were there too and then he and Mangy Tom disappeared.

At midnight Pa's alarm had just gone off when Sherpa appeared outside again. He called quietly, "There's someone in the showground."

Jake called back, "Pa will be out in a minute with Brian." He looked down at Brian who nodded to show that he had heard what Sherpa had said. Sherpa disappeared again, just as Pa emerged from the bedroom.

"Come on Brian," he said quietly. "Duty calls." And he and Brian silently set out from the caravan, Pa shutting the door carefully behind him, not giving the cats any chance to slip out with them.

Brian ran ahead of Pa looking around to see if he could catch a glimpse of the person Sherpa had seen, but the showground seemed still and empty and he wasn't sure which way to go.

Suddenly he heard his name being called from behind one of the stalls. He slipped round quickly and found Sherpa behind the stall looking very agitated.

"What's wrong?" Brian asked quietly.

Sherpa shook his head. "I don't know. I'm sure I can hear water."

Brian listened carefully. His sharp ears caught the noise Sherpa had heard.

"It sounds like a tap running." They looked at each other in alarm.

"The field tap!" exclaimed Sherpa. "Quick! Lead Pa over to that side of the field."

Brian returned to Pa and started barking. Then he turned and raced towards the tap, which had been fitted by the farmer halfway down one side of the field, to water the cattle when they were in there. As Brian got near to it, he could see that the tap had been turned full on and water was cascading all over the ground. The area was beginning to flood.

When Pa caught up, he started towards the tap to turn it off, only to find himself wading through inches of water. He managed to get to the tap and turn it off and then, keeping Brian close beside him, he looked round the rest of the showground, although he felt sure that, whoever had turned the tap on, was long gone. He shone his torch round the area to see how bad the flooding was and was relieved to see that the tap had obviously not been running for long.

When Pa and Brian got back to the caravan, Ma was waiting up for them. The cats had been unsettled and had disturbed her. As soon as she saw Pa's face, she knew something was wrong. As he squelched into the caravan, she looked in amazement at his wet and rather muddy feet.

"What on earth's happened?" she asked.

Pa eased his feet out of his sopping slippers and said, "Someone turned the field tap full on. It can't have been done many minutes before I got there. The ground around the tap was

flooded but no further. Brian led me to it, good lad that he is."
He turned and patted the big dog.

"Is there any damage done?" Ma asked anxiously.

Pa shook his head. "It'll be a bit boggy round the tap for a
while, but the sun will dry it out pretty quickly. However, if we
hadn't found it so soon and it had been running for hours, the
whole of that side of the showground, including the tents and
stalls, would have been flooded. It's a good job we stayed
overnight."

"And a good job we had Brian with us," added Ma, who had
already reached for the kettle and was, of course, in the
process of making a cup of tea. Pa went into the bedroom to
clean up and find some dry pyjama trousers and, by the time
he came out, Ma had the tea ready.

"Do you think we ought to keep checking the tap?" she asked.

Pa shook his head. "They won't come back. I don't suppose
they know we're sleeping here. They'll assume the tap is
still on."

They took their cups of tea back into the bedroom and the
animals settled in the living area to talk quietly.

"Well done, Brian," said Jake.

"It wasn't me," admitted Brian honestly. "Sherpa was waiting
for us behind one of the stalls and said he could hear water.
We realised it must be the field tap and so I led Pa to it."

Libby smiled at him. "It's a good job you did. If that tap had
been running all night, it would have flooded half the
showground and it would probably have meant the show

wouldn't be able to go ahead. They'd never have got it sorted in time."

Jake became aware of movement outside. He looked out of the window and saw Sherpa. The other three Spy Club patrollers were hiding in the shadows. Sherpa came forward and said quietly, "We're going home now. I don't think whoever it is will come back again and it will be getting light in a couple of hours anyway."

Jake nodded. "Okay. We'll talk about it tomorrow. Thanks all of you. Take care."

The four shadows disappeared and Jake turned to the others. "They've gone home. It seems safe enough for now. I think Sherpa's right. Whoever it is won't come back now. Come on, let's get some sleep."

The five animals settled themselves comfortably and were all soon fast asleep. Ma and Pa lay talking for some time before they eventually managed to get back to sleep. They had a horrible feeling that the vandal hadn't finished with the show yet and they wondered what they could expect next.

CHAPTER EIGHT

Everyone woke early on Friday morning. While Ma made breakfast Pa and Brian did a quick check of the showground, but all was well. The area around the tap was still boggy but the early morning sun was already starting to dry it out.

After breakfast Ma, Pa and the animals went to the tea tent to set up for the day. Ma had just got the tea urn switched on when the Colonel came in accompanied by two members of the committee, Geoff and another man called Sam. While Ma made tea for everyone Pa told them about the events of the night. All three men were horrified at the thought of what might have happened if the tap had been left running.

"Thank goodness you were here and checking the place," said the Colonel.

They sat down to drink their tea and, as more helpers arrived and were told the news, the noise in the tent rose. All of them were both shocked and angered that the vandal was continuing their feud against the village show. But however much they thought about and discussed it, no-one could think who might be doing it or come up with a reason for someone to try to stop the show going ahead.

The usual clanking announced the arrival of Mad Mary's Land Rover and she came rushing into the tent – Ma had phoned to tell her what had happened. She was so upset that she had apparently forgotten to put Tarran on his lead. Strangely, though, he walked in quite quietly, followed by a smirking Max. Tarran, looking fed up, settled by his post and Max joined Jake and the others.

"What's so funny?" Jake asked Max. Not a lot made Max laugh, so it must be something good.

Max smirk grew wider. "Mad Mary was in such a state she forgot to let us out. I jumped out of the window. Dopey, here, was in such a hurry to jump out of the other window, he didn't remember to check that it was open. Bashed his nose on the glass." He started laughing. The animals looked at Tarran, who was clearly feeling rather silly, and all joined in Max`s laughter.

Eventually kind Libby said, "Never mind Tarran. We all do silly things sometimes. Come over and sit with us, since Mad Mary's forgotten to tie you up."

Max gave a huge long-suffering sigh but said nothing. The others made room for Tarran and he went over to join them, feeling much more cheerful. It was the first time he had been included in the group and it made him wonder if eventually they might be willing to be friends with him. Mad Mary noticed him move and made as if to go over and put him on his lead but, when she saw him sitting with the others looking perfectly calm, she decided to leave him where he was and see how he behaved.

When the helpers went back to work, the animals followed them out. Tarran hung back, not sure if he would be allowed to go, but Max said, "Come on, Tarran. Show everyone that you can behave like a sensible dog."

Tarran rushed to join them and was out of the tent before Mad Mary realised what was happening. She was about to go after him when Ma stopped her. "Let him go. The others will keep an eye on him. If he causes any bother someone will let you know quick enough."

The animals went to look at the area around the tap, which had almost dried out. Then they went to the food area, the other side of the tea tent. The food vans were arriving and taking their usual places. They went over to look at the newly painted stalls, which glowed brightly in the sun. People were bringing things to start setting up, although most would be brought the following morning. The show would start at midday. The showground was filled with busy, excited people, working hard to make a success of the show named for their villages. It was a matter of pride with them that the person or people vandalising the show ground didn't win. It was a feeling all the animals shared.

After having had a good look round and chatting to a couple of visiting cats and a dog and telling them all about the events of the night, the animals made their way back to the tea tent. Tarran had been quite subdued and so no message had gone back to Mad Mary telling her to tie up her dog! The other animals were beginning to get used to having him around.

Just after lunch, much to their surprise, Sherpa turned up at the showground. He stayed out of sight but called to the animals from outside the tent and they went out, wondering what had brought him to the showground in the daytime. They had expected him to sleep most of the day ready for his night-time patrol. However, one look at him showed that he had something important that he wanted to tell them.

Jake led them all behind the tea tent, where they would be out of sight of prying eyes. Sherpa went and sat by Ginny who said, "Why are you here so early, Sherpa? What's up?"

Sherpa frowned. "Something you should know. The figure I saw last night. It was a woman and she looked familiar to me.

I don't know why. I asked Tom but he hadn't seen her face. It's really bugging me but I'm sure I've seen her before."

The other animals were all surprised that the vandal was apparently a lone woman. "Why do you think she's familiar?" asked Libby.

"Maybe she lives in one of the villages," suggested Jake.

Sherpa shook his head. "I don't think so. I just can't put my paw on what it is about her that's familiar."

"What did she look like?" asked Libby.

"She had blonde, straggly hair and was about Ma's height and size. I didn't really see anything else. It was too dark and she was gone too quickly. She had a torch, which was how I managed to get a bit of a look at her face."

Jake looked serious. "We'll have to be extra vigilant tonight. Pa will probably do several checks, but we really need as many on patrol as we can manage. We need to have someone out there all the time."

Sherpa nodded. "Mangy Tom's gone to round up as many of the team as he can find. Beelzebub and Leo will be here again, as soon as it gets dark. I'll stay here now and wait for them."

"Please be careful tonight," said Ginny. She couldn't help but remember how Sherpa had risked his life the last time.

"Don't worry." said Sherpa reassuringly. "If we see anyone, we'll come straight to the caravan to alert Pa. Now I'm going to find a shady spot and have a nap. I'll see you later." And he got up and wandered out of sight.

"Well, what do you think?" Jake asked the others. They all looked puzzled. Libby said, "It must be someone reasonably local or how else would Sherpa have thought she was familiar?"

"It could be someone who visits or has visited the area," suggested Ginny.

"Yes, that's possible," agreed Wesley, "but it still doesn't explain why they are attacking the villages' show. What could have happened to make them feel like that?"

The animals looked at each other but no-one could think of a reason.

For the rest of the afternoon they sat quietly outside the tea tent, watching the activity going on around them. They were all thinking of the coming night and wondering and worrying about what nasty tricks they could expect from the unknown attacker.

CHAPTER NINE

In the early evening, once the showground had emptied, Ma and Pa quickly ate their tea and then, accompanied by Brian and the four cats, they did a thorough search of the showground. Both humans and animals looked at everything with a sense of satisfaction at what had been achieved, in spite of the attempts of the vandal to spoil things. From what Sherpa had told Jake and the others, it seemed likely that there was only one person involved, and that person was a woman.

Ma and Pa sat outside the tea tent again, until it began to get dark, but the animals settled behind the tea tent this time, out of sight, where they met up with Sherpa again. A couple of minutes later Mangy Tom also turned up and said that Beelzebub, Leo, Sooty and Patch would definitely be there by the time it got dark. Lucy Locket and Fred also hoped to be there at some point. Between them they would patrol all areas of the showground. They had heard Pa telling Ma he planned to do a check of the showground every hour.

"Hopefully that should be enough," said Jake. "Anything out of the ordinary, don't try any heroics, report back straightaway."

"Yes Sir!" said Sherpa, making them all smile, although every one of them was feeling anxious, convinced that something else would happen during the night. Mangy Tom then went off to mooch about by himself until it was time to meet the others. Sherpa looked at Ginny and winked. "Fancy a walk, Girl?" and the two of them went off, keeping out of sight of Ma and Pa who would wonder why Sherpa was there.

Half an hour later Ginny appeared alone and said Sherpa had gone to wait by the car park entrance, where he had arranged to meet the others.

"When can we expect wedding bells then?" asked Wesley cheekily and got a cuff round the ear from Ginny, although she only just managed to hide a satisfied smile.

To her surprise Jake spoke up. "He's a good lad, Sherpa. I misjudged him." There had been a time when Jake had looked down on the big grey tabby because he was one of a litter of farm cats. The events of the past couple of months had shown him how wrong he had been!

Brian nodded and Libby said, "We've learnt a lot about our fellow animals since we've been dabbling in crime fighting."

"And our fellow humans," added Jake, thinking to himself that there were some really horrible humans around, like the woman doing her best to ruin the show. But then they were balanced by kind people like Mr Browning and John, the rope man, who had put themselves out to try to help.

By then it was beginning to get dark, and Ma and Pa appeared, making their way back to the caravan. Pa set his alarm for an hour ahead and he and Ma went to the bedroom for Pa to get what sleep he could. The animals settled in their usual places and, in spite of their concern about the possible activities of the vandal, they were all soon drifting off to sleep.

Suddenly, Jake was woken by a noise outside the caravan. As he peered into the darkness outside, he could just see Mangy Tom pacing up and down in a very agitated way.

With a feeling of dread, he shouted, "What's up?" startling all the occupants of the caravan, human and animal.

"You've got to come quickly!" Tom yelled back. "One of the tents is on fire, on the far side of the field."

"What!" Jake gasped, appalled.

"What is it?" asked Libby, anxiously. "What's the matter?"

Jake turned to the others. "Tom says there's a tent on fire."

The noise the animals were making had woken Ma and Pa, and Pa came sleepily into the living area, pulling on his dressing gown.

"What's up with you lot?" he said, frowning.

"Come on! You've got to find a way to get out." shouted Tom. His yowling attracted Pa's attention and he stared out of the window. He could see a black and white cat pacing up and down outside the caravan and he immediately recognised the stray he had noticed several times with his own cats. He looked closely at the restless cat and then back at the five agitated animals staring out of the window. As one they turned to look at Pa, trying to impress upon him the urgency of the situation.

For weeks Pa had been trying to convince himself that there was nothing strange about the animals' behaviour; domestic animals just didn't form gangs and work together. If you looked at it logically, there was a simple common-sense explanation for everything they did.

Now, looking from the stray to the anxious faces of his own animals, he thought about the times he'd seen groups of cats at the top of the garden, he thought of the night they had been present and apparently acting together when the two burglars had been caught. And he gave up on logic and common sense.

There was now no doubt in his mind that the stray had brought a message to the caravan and, whatever it was, it was urgent. He looked again at the five faces staring at him in frustration. He looked again at the pacing stray outside. Whatever was urgent the cats and Brian knew what it was and he didn't.

And so he opened the caravan door!

All five animals raced out of the caravan and followed Mangy Tom, who was already round the tea tent and tearing back across the field.

Ma had come out of the bedroom in time to see Pa opening the caravan door and the animals racing out and away.

"What are you doing, Pa? Don't let them out. They'll get lost in the dark."

Pa grabbed a torch and his mobile and set off after the fast-disappearing animals. "Don't worry," he called back to Ma. "I'll stay with them. Something's up."

And he disappeared into the dark, trusting that the animals would lead him to the problem. Ma turned to pull on her dressing gown and slippers, struggling with both she was in such a hurry. Then she followed her now out-of-sight husband and animals.

By the time Pa had rounded the tea tent, Jake and the others were more than halfway across the field. On the far side they could see an orange glow at the back of one of the competition tents. Suddenly, three cats raced towards them from the direction of the fire – Sherpa, Beelzebub and Leo had been with Mangy Tom when he discovered the fire.

"Quick, quick!" said Sherpa breathlessly. "There's someone in there, lying on the floor."

As they reached the tent, they could see the far side of it ablaze. Through the front opening they could see some of the tables, near to the side of the tent on fire, were starting to catch fire themselves and, lying on the floor by the side of one of the smouldering tables, was the figure of an elderly man.

Without a second thought, Brian raced into the tent and grabbed the man's trouser leg. Tugging with all his might he slowly started to drag the man towards the opening of the tent, ignoring the sparks of fire dropping onto his coat. Unable to help, the cats gathered by the entrance, shouting encouragement to the brave dog.

As Brian got the man near to the opening, Pa arrived, speaking into his mobile. Running after the animals he had seen the orange glow and, his heart sinking, had realised immediately what it meant and had phoned the fire brigade.

As he reached the group of yowling cats, he saw with horror the figure being dragged by the tiring dog. Pushing his way through the crowd of cats, he grabbed the old man's other leg, and he and Brian pulled the unconscious figure outside to safety. As soon as they were far enough from the burning tent Pa was on his phone again, this time for an ambulance and the police.

As he was talking to the Emergency Services operator, Ma puffed up to them. Her eyes filled with tears as she looked at the burning tent. Then she saw the figure lying on the grass and immediately went over and knelt down beside him, listening as Pa spoke on his mobile.

The cats and Brian crowded together, horrified at what had happened. Libby and Ginny stood by Brian, licking his coat where the sparks had singed it. They all looked in despair at the scene of destruction in front of them. Not only would the tent be burnt beyond use, but all the produce, which people had proudly displayed on the tables, would be ruined as well.

Jake was the first to recover. "Well done, Brian," he said, rubbing against the weary dog. "That was very brave of you."

The other cats joined in with their own congratulations, all except Mangy Tom. He had gone over to the old man to have a closer look and came back to the others looking very concerned. Sherpa noticed his serious look and said, "What is it, Tom? What's up?"

"Do you know who it is?" replied Tom.

The other animals moved to have a look at the figure, but all came back shaking their heads. None of them remembered seeing the old man before.

"It's Old Joe Finnegan." Tom's words made all the other stare at him in disbelief.

"Melanie's grandfather?" Libby asked, appalled. Melanie was one of the burglars who had targeted the villages earlier in the year.

"That woman I saw!" exclaimed Sherpa. "I knew she looked familiar."

"But Melanie's in custody still," said Ginny. "It couldn't be her, could it? You don't think she's got out?"

Sherpa shook his head. "No, the woman was too old to be Melanie. She was middle aged. But I bet she's related to her in some way."

Their conversation was interrupted by the sound of a siren and, looking towards the road, they saw flashing blue lights as a fire engine raced towards the showground. Almost immediately the sound of more sirens filled the air and an ambulance and a police car appeared at the showground entrance. The vehicle drivers had no need to ask where to go. The tent was well alight and would be clearly visible to those living in the villages closest to the showground. To the concern of everyone, humans and animals, the sparks flying about meant there was a danger that the fire would spread to the stalls and tents nearby.

Within seconds the firemen were tackling the blazing tent with the greatest efficiency and the paramedics were attending to Joe, still lying unconscious on the grass.

"Let's go back to the caravan." suggested Jake. "There's nothing more we can do here and we'll only be in the way."

The animals melted into the darkness and made their way back to the tea tent, meeting the four other patrollers on the way. They had gone to look for the vandal, in the hope that whoever it was hadn't left the showground.

"Any sign of her?" asked Jake.

Sooty shook her head. "We just managed to catch sight of a car going off up the lane, but it was too quick for us to make out what kind or colour it was."

"It was going towards Littlebury," added Lucy Locket, "so maybe the firemen saw it."

Jake sighed. "It's a thought but how can we ask them?" Once again, they came up against the problem of communication.

When they got back to the caravan the door was open. In her rush Ma had forgotten to shut it. However, the cats decided to go into the tea tent – the caravan would be a bit cramped with a big dog and so many cats.

Once they had settled everyone looked at Jake.

"Well," said Libby, "what now?"

Jake looked perplexed. "To be honest, I don't know. If Sherpa's right, it seems to me that one of Melanie's relatives is causing all the damage. I imagine they're taking revenge on the villagers for what happened to Melanie by trying to wreck the show."

Wesley looked slightly uncomfortable. "You don't think Old Joe has got something to do with it. He *was* here after dark."

The others looked horrified at the thought, but Sherpa shook his head. "When Tom and I found him in the tent the back of his head was bleeding, as if someone had hit him."

All the animals looked at Sherpa, disbelief written across all their faces. Libby was the first one able to speak. "And they set fire to the tent and left him there!"

"Seems to me," said Mangy Tom, in a tone of voice none of the others had ever heard him use before, "that this situation is getting serious. If something's not done soon, we might be too late next time." It appeared that even carefree Tom was beginning to be concerned about what was happening.

Libby nodded but looked confused. "But what was Old Joe doing here in the first place? Do you think whoever is doing this is trying to harm him as well?" She gave a frustrated sigh.

"If only we had a way of letting the humans know what we think is going on."

Jake smiled briefly. "Well, I can't think of a way of doing that exactly, but I do think we now have a human ally."

All the cats looked at Jake as if he were mad. Brian simply nodded. "Pa!" he said.

"Pa!" said Ginny, astonished. "How do you make that out?"

Jake looked at Brian. "You saw him too?"

Brian nodded again. "He looked at Mangy Tom and then at us and he knew. He knew Tom had brought an urgent message to us and that's when he opened the door."

To begin with the others found the idea too incredible to accept. Wesley was the first of the others to start believing what Jake and Brian were saying. "You know, he's been watching us a lot since the burglaries, looking puzzled."

All the animals started talking at once so that Ma and Pa, returning to the tea tent, walked into a caterwauling of yowls and barks.

Ma looked worried. "They've really been upset by all this."

Pa nodded. "Go and get dressed. We'll need to get the tea on. I'll look after the animals."

Ma went to go but then looked again at the animals and suddenly seemed to take in the number of cats sitting there.

"What on earth…! Where have all these cats come from? That's Sherpa and Beelzebub and Marcus's cat. Why are they here and who are the others?"

Pa thought quickly. "They've probably been hanging around all day. You know cats." Ma stood looking at the cats for a second or two, but then gave a nod although she didn't look convinced. Pa gave her a little push.

"Go and get dressed. The others will be coming here soon and we need to have hot drinks to give them."

The thought of people needing to be supplied with hot drinks distracted Ma from the cats and she made her way back to the caravan. Pa turned and looked hard at the animals in front of him and they all looked back at him.

"Well done, Brian." he said, giving the big dog a pat. "You probably saved Old Joe's life. You and this gang of cats." Then he added, "It's a good job you were on patrol." His voice was saying 'I'm joking', but the way he looked at them all said, `I know what you're doing`.

Jake went over to him and rubbed against his leg. It was the only way he could think of to thank Pa for opening the caravan door. Pa bent down and stroked him.

"If only he could understand us!" said Libby wistfully.

The same thought was obviously going through Pa's mind. "If only you could talk." he said. "But never mind, we'll manage, we'll manage alright."

And in that moment, by unspoken agreement, Pa became an honorary member of Jake's Spy Club.

CHAPTER TEN

The next few hours were full of activity and noise coming from the area round the burnt tent. To the cats, left sitting in the tea tent, it sounded very loud and confusing, but they saw later that, however chaotic it had sounded, there was nothing chaotic about the results. The firemen had certainly shown how expert they were at their job. They had managed to put out the tent on fire quite speedily and had made absolutely sure none of the nearby stalls and tents were in any danger.

The Spy Club patrollers, except for Sherpa, had gone home, all planning to get some sleep to be ready for whatever the vandal would have lined up for Saturday night. The events of the night had shown them that they would need all their wits about them to deal with whatever the vandal had planned to do next.

Jake, Sherpa and the other three were left alone with Brian so that, when Ma returned to the tent, she almost believed she had imagined the mass of cats she had seen. She looked hard at Sherpa but said nothing. She knew from her elderly next-door neighbour, Arthur, who was Sherpa's owner, that he was inclined to wander at night.

After his conversation with the cats, Pa had gone to get dressed and then he and Ma had started getting hot drinks prepared. Pa had phoned some of the committee members and they had come straight to the showground, arriving as the firefighters were beginning to pack up their equipment.

The Colonel and the other committee members looked at the ruined tent with a mixture of horror, disgust and despair. The tent had been where the vegetable and produce competitions would be held and many of the entries had already been put out, all of them now destroyed or damaged beyond repair.

Old Joe had been taken off to hospital. Sherpa had been right – he had an injury to the back of his head - but the police told Ma that it had been an accident. To the relief of the animals Old Joe had not been attacked by the woman apparently causing all the damage. He had briefly regained consciousness before being taken off to hospital and told the paramedics and police that he had seen someone going into the back entrance of the tent. He followed them in and saw them pouring liquid over the entries on the tables. He shouted at them and they turned and ran out through the front. As Joe made to go after them, he had caught his foot, fallen and hit his head on one of the wooden tables.

The police sergeant who came to investigate, Sergeant Brown, told Ma this but when she asked what Old Joe was doing at the showground at night the sergeant simply shrugged. "We asked him, but he passed out again before he could tell us."

The firemen and police had come to the tea tent to talk to Pa and the others and welcomed the plentiful cups of tea and coffee that Ma was providing. She had wanted to put Brian and the cats back in the caravan, but Pa stopped her.

"They'll be more settled here with us." And Ma let them stay.

"Good old Pa," thought the animals. "He knows we want to hear what's said."

When Sergeant Brown and his constable arrived at the tent, the animals noticed that the constable was PC Watkins, the sympathetic officer who had dealt with the other incidents. The sergeant was very serious, having been told by the Chief

Fire Officer that the fire had definitely been started deliberately. He turned to the villagers and said, "There must be something behind these acts of vandalism. Have you no idea who might have a grudge against the villages or the show?"

It was clear that the police were now taking the vandalism much more seriously. Damage to ropes and stalls was one thing, but arson was another matter altogether. Especially when lives were put at risk.

Pa, Ma and the others all looked completely baffled. The animals gazed at each other in despair. They were sure they knew the answer but how could they pass on that information to the humans? They all concentrated hard trying to pass their thoughts into Pa's head, but it didn't work. Pa showed no sign of having a sudden flash of inspiration.

Eventually the firefighters and the police left the showground and the committee members started discussing how they were going to deal with the situation. By four o' clock villagers started arriving to help – the village grapevine had been at work – and the serious business of sorting things out really got started. The Colonel was attempting to find something to replace the burnt tent and others were finding replacement tables and speaking to people whose entries had been destroyed to see if they could provide more.

It was still very early in the morning, but they only had a few hours to get everything ready for the opening of the show and nobody seemed to mind being woken so early. The Summer Show was close to all the villagers' hearts and they were happy to do anything to ensure its success.

The animals, feeling there was nothing to be gained by hanging about, settled in a corner of the tea tent to listen to the conversations of the people who came to the tent to grab a quick drink. They learnt nothing new but listened in complete agreement to people saying what they'd like to happen to the vandal if or when they caught them.

At six o' clock they heard Mad Mary's Land Rover rattle up and, a few moments later, Max appeared in the tea tent closely followed by Mad Mary with two dogs on leads – one was Tarran and the other was Old Joe's dog, Bruiser. Mad Mary tied them up near to Jake and the others and went to join Ma.

The cats and dogs all started to talk at once and the noise was deafening. Eventually Jake stood up and all the animals went silent. Speaking to Max he said, "I suppose you know what's happened?"

Max nodded. "Ma phoned Mad Mary. That's why Bruiser is with us. Mad Mary went to get him when she found out about Old Joe."

The animals all looked sympathetically at Bruiser, who was lying down looking miserable.

"We think we know who's doing it!" blurted out Wesley.

Max opened his eyes wide, looking rather impressed. "Really? You seem to be getting very good at this spy business. So, who is it?"

Jake sighed. "We don't know exactly who, but we think it's one of Melanie's relatives, out to get revenge."

Sherpa butted in. "I said that woman I saw looked familiar. When they said the old man was Melanie's grandfather, I realised whom she reminded me of."

"We think she must be a relative who blames the villagers for what happened to Melanie." said Libby. "I don't suppose she really meant any harm to come to Melanie's grandfather, though."

"Not her grandfather," mumbled Bruiser.

"What!" shouted Jake and then lowered his voice as some of the humans, disturbed by his loud yowl, stared at the animals. "What was she doing at his house if she wasn't his granddaughter?"

"Step granddaughter," replied Bruiser. "Marge was married before and had a daughter, Maggie." Marge was Old Joe's wife who had died a few years earlier.

"Melanie is Maggie's daughter," continued Bruiser. "Like mother, like daughter. Both nasty."

The animals all looked at each other. "Do you think it could be her?" asked Sherpa. "She looked about the right age. When Old Joe interrupted her putting stuff on the vegetable entries, she probably thought she'd better get out before he recognised her. I expect she went back later to set the tent on fire not knowing he was still in there."

"Wouldn't put it past her," said Bruiser. "Like I said, nasty, and she and Joe never did get on."

"So," said Max, "we have a fairly good idea about who is doing this and why. Now, how do we get this information across to the humans?"

Jake gave a mischievous smile. "We work on Pa, the newest member of Spy Club!"

For once Max looked taken aback. "I'm sure you're going to explain that rather strange comment."

With help from the others, Jake told Max, Tarran and Bruiser about the events of the evening and how they had gradually realised that Pa was on to them.

"Well," said Max eventually. "I suppose that helps, but we still haven't got a way of telling Pa. Unless you're going to tell me he's done a crash course in cat language."

"We wish!" said Wesley and the gang of animals laughed, causing the humans to look across at them again.

"They're getting restless," said Ma.

Just then Claire and Simon appeared at the entrance, Claire looking rather tearful. "Oh Ma, isn't it awful? Who could be so mean?"

Before she had a chance to say anything else, Brian rushed over to her, licking her hand and demanding her attention. She looked lovingly at the big dog.

"And you, young man. I've heard all about how you saved Old Joe from the fire. My brave boy."

She and Simon fussed over Brian for a few moments and then went to join Ma and Mad Mary, saying, "What are we going to do?"

Ma looked rather pleased with things and said, "We think we've got it sorted. The Colonel has been wonderful and, yet again, worked his magic. He's arranged for some marquees to replace the tent. He's also arranged for two of the village halls to lend us some tables."

The Colonel went rather pink at Ma's praise. She continued, "We've contacted all the people who had entries in the tent and all of them can provide replacements. They won't be their best, of course, but nobody seems to mind. They all want to help show this horrible person they won't win."

She stood up and turned to Claire and Simon. "Would you stay with the tea urn and serve anyone who comes in, while Mary and I go and help get things ready for midday?" Determined to be optimistic she added, "There's a lot to do but we've well over five hours to go. Plenty of time. We'll get it all ready, don't you worry."

Claire said she could manage on her own and sent Simon to help wherever he could. He had taken a break from his work when he'd heard about the fire and had come to the showground with Claire to see what he could do to help. Now he went off with the others, all determined to do whatever was necessary to make sure that this year's Valley Villages Summer Show was the success it had always been.

CHAPTER ELEVEN

Once the tent had cleared all the animals looked at Jake to see what he thought they should do next. Jake sat up tall and said firmly, "We're going to have to patrol the showground all day and all night. If this woman is prepared to set fire to things, there's no knowing what she'll do. So far everything has been done at night but now, with the show actually on, she may try a bit of daytime disruption. In fact, I'm sure she will."

Libby looked unsure. "How are we going to manage to do all that? Two and a half days and two nights. Will there be enough of us?"

"Some of us will have to do certain times. Mrs Whittacker always brings Toby to the show on the Sunday so he can patrol then. Those who can do nights will stick with that. We'll have to get Mangy Tom to go delivering messages again, getting as many of the club as he can to come, day or night."

Before he could go on Mangy Tom himself appeared in the tent. He had decided to stay nearby and had been waiting until the humans had left.

"So what's been arranged?" he asked.

They told him what they had planned and he nodded his approval. He wandered over to where Ma was dealing with the tea urn and looked at her hopefully. Again, she looked hard at him, recognising the stray Libby had once brought home, but, again, she said nothing. She rummaged around in one of her bags and found him some cat biscuits, which he polished off in no time and then disappeared out of the tent calling, "See you later," to the other animals.

Wesley, getting back to business, said, "What about Bruiser? Hadn't he better stay in here, just in case?"

Jake nodded. "Good thinking, Wesley. We had better leave him under Ma's watchful eye. You never know whether the woman will try to hurt him to get at Old Joe. But everyone else will be on patrol at some point. Even the night patrollers, if they can manage it, should try to be at the showground for some time while the show's on."

When Jake had finished there was the sound of a plaintive whine. They all looked at Tarran, who had edged as close to the group as he could.

"What's up with you?" asked Max, not unkindly.

Tarran looked at the others and said pleadingly, "Can't I do something to help? I know I'm not a member of Spy Club, but couldn't I do something?"

The animals all looked at each other. They appreciated his willingness to help, but wondered if they could trust him to behave sensibly. Tarran looked at them all anxiously. He was desperate to be able to join in, but he knew he hadn't exactly shown himself to be reliable. The animals all looked at each other doubtfully.

Eventually Max looked at Jake and said, "Your decision."

Jake looked at Tarran and saw how much the young dog wanted to help. He said firmly, "If we let you help, will you be sensible and do as you're told?"

Tarran nodded eagerly. "Promise. I don't mean to be naughty. No-one's ever told me how to behave."

"What about your previous owners?" asked Brian. "Didn't they train you?" Brian had been taken to Puppy Training classes by Claire and he had assumed that all owners did that.

"I was owned by an old man who died a few weeks after I went to live with him," said Tarran. "His family didn't want me and threw me out. I'd been a stray for quite a long time before Mad Mary took me in."

The animals looked at Tarran, absolutely horrified at the story they had just heard. All the animals had had loving, caring homes all their lives and what they had heard explained a lot about Tarran. Suddenly he didn't seem so bad.

Jake smiled. "Okay, you're in. You'll have to make sure you get Mad Mary to let you off your lead. Then you can patrol with Max."

Tarran got quite excited at the thought of working with the Spy Club animals, then remembered he was supposed to be showing them how sensible he could be, so he sat down and tried to look like a well-behaved, self-controlled dog.

Max looked rather resigned but accepted his role as Tarran's minder with a good grace. After all, they needed all the help they could get and everyone knew that, if anyone could keep Tarran in line, it would be Max. They would just have to make sure they stopped Mad Mary from tying him up.

"Well," said Wesley breezily. "Two new recruits to Jake's Spy Club in one day. We *are* doing well." And the group of animals laughed and felt a little more relaxed.

It was decided that the animals would patrol in pairs, each pair concentrating on one area. As they were unable to patrol during the night, during the day Jake would patrol the tents with Libby, Brian and Wesley the area by the carpark, toilets and food vans. The stalls would be checked by Max and Tarran and Ginny would keep an eye on the show rings with Sherpa, who offered to do both days and nights and catch what sleep he could.

Everyone knew that finding the woman was only the start of their problems but, for now, they would have to concentrate on that. Feeling sure that nothing was likely to happen before the show started, they all settled down to sleep while they could consider themselves off duty.

When they woke up there was half an hour to go before the show was to be opened by the Colonel, so, having to leave poor Tarran tied up with Bruiser, who was still asleep snoring loudly, they went to have a final stroll round to see what had been done.

They were amazed at what they saw. The villagers had really worked a miracle. The burnt tent had been taken down and taken away, along with the damaged trestle tables and burnt produce. Two small marquees had been put side by side and the village hall tables laid out inside. Competitors had raided their gardens to find replacement entries. Fortunately, the final judging wouldn't take place until Monday. The whole showground looked sparkling and ready.

The animals sat together to watch the Colonel give his thank you speech, in which he referred to the various incidents and thanked the villagers for working together to overcome the problems that had been caused.

The little pack of animals drew interested stares from people. They were used to seeing animals wandering the showground but not usually in such numbers. However, fortunately, once the show was opened, they lost interest in the animals and went off to enjoy themselves.

The afternoon passed uneventfully. The sharp-eyed animals had seen no sign of a woman resembling Melanie or anyone looking shifty in any way. The stalls did well and the villagers seemed pleased with how the day had ended, considering how badly it had started. They were able to congratulate themselves on successfully turning disaster into triumph.

When the animals gathered together to report back at the end of the first day, they felt a mixture of pleasure and relief that they had had no disasters to deal with. Wesley and Brian had had a particularly good afternoon. The area they patrolled included the food vans and they had found the food vendors very friendly and generous! Not surprisingly, at the end of the day when Ma fed the animals, neither of them had felt hungry!

An added bonus was that Mad Mary had gone for a walk around the showground and taken Tarran with her, off his lead. She had noticed that he had been a lot quieter and decided to risk it. He had behaved perfectly, well aware that his chances of being able to help patrol the showground the following day relied on him showing Mad Mary that he was to be trusted.

When they returned to the tea tent he got a satisfied nod from Max, who had been watching him, and he knew that he had passed the test. Mad Mary's praise when she got him back was very welcome, but it didn't mean as much to him as the slight, approving nod that Max gave him.

Pa was planning to do his regular patrols every hour and two men on the committee had promised to come and look round a couple of times during the night. Leo, Beelzebub, Sooty and

Patch were to do the first night's patrol for the animals and had all promised to stay around during the day to help out.

However, for some reason, Jake was convinced that no more acts of vandalism would take place during the night. He was sure that, whatever was to be done, it would be done while the show was on.

Jake was proved to be right the following morning when nothing had happened to disturb the peace of the night. As it started to get light Beelzebub and the others came to the caravan to say they were going to find somewhere to sleep and would be around later in the day.

They were just leaving when Pa and Brian came back from what Pa had decided would be their final patrol of the night. He looked at the four cats disappearing into the undergrowth nearby and then at his own cats sitting looking out of the caravan window watching them go. He simply nodded at them as he and Brian entered the caravan and then went off to get some sleep before the day's work started.

CHAPTER TWELVE

Sunday morning dawned bright and sunny and, as people arrived to get the showground ready for the expected visitors, there was a feeling of excitement and expectation, shared by the animals.

Mad Mary arrived early, closely followed by Claire. To the animals' great relief, Mad Mary had walked in followed by Max and Tarran, no longer on his lead. They joined the other animals in their usual place at the side of the tea tent.

"Where's Bruiser?" asked Jake. He had expected the old dog to be with them.

"Mad Mary thought he looked tired, so she's left him at home," replied Max. "He's shut in the house and she'll go back a couple of times to let him out. He's probably safer there than here."

The rest of the animals agreed and were pleased not to have the added worry of keeping a watch on Bruiser.

The show was due to start at ten and by then the car park was almost full and people were queuing to get in. There was a buzz of noise as the visitors, full of a sense of excitement and anticipation, chatted to each other as they waited.

At ten o' clock the attendants by the gates opened them up and the crowds swarmed into the showground. People came from miles around to attend the show and soon there was the sound of excited laughter and chatter around the showground.

Sergeant Brown and PC Watkins were there patrolling the showground, but clearly not quite sure who or what they were looking out for. The animals felt frustrated that they couldn't point them in the right direction. However, they wandered round in their pairs, enjoying the buzz but keeping a sharp lookout for anything out of the ordinary. They tended to look particularly closely at middle-aged women with blonde hair!

They had been joined by Toby, the sprightly Jack Russell, who had been a late addition to Spy Club but who had proved himself to be a real asset. He was at the show with his owner, Mrs Whittacker, but she was used to him wandering off on his own and he was able to stroll round the showground, chatting to the other Spy Club members when he met them but with his sharp eyes taking everything in. He had thoroughly enjoyed his involvement with the Spy Club animals in July. It had livened up his rather dull life and he was delighted that he was now an accepted and respected member of the club.

The morning passed uneventfully and the animals relaxed a bit. They spent most of their time casually sauntering round. If they'd been humans, they would have had their hands in their pockets and be whistling tunelessly! But, in spite of their apparently aimless wandering, they made sure they regularly covered every inch of their area of the showground and their eyes missed nothing. The night patrollers took it in turns to sit behind the tea tent and snooze for twenty minutes or so. Sherpa's first twenty minutes became an hour, but nobody minded. He'd more than done his share.

Early in the afternoon Jake and Libby, having just had a break in the tea tent, were beginning to make their way back to the craft tent to have another look round, when they saw Sherpa racing towards them across the showground. When he got to them, he stopped to get his breath and then said urgently,

"That woman I saw the other night. She's here. She's hanging round the dog show rings."

Jake and Libby exchanged glances. "What do we do?" asked Libby anxiously.

"Can you go round the showground and tell all the others to make their way to the show rings?" Jake asked her. "We've got to keep a watch on her. She's obviously up to something."

Libby nodded and raced off. Jake turned to Sherpa and asked anxiously, "Where's Ginny?"

"She's keeping an eye on the woman," answered Sherpa. "It's okay, she's not on her own. Toby's there as well. Come on let's get back."

The two cats raced across the showground, dodging around people's feet and causing more than one person to scold them.

When they got to the two show rings, they could see Ginny and Toby by the side of the bigger of the two rings.

"Where is she?" asked Jake when they got within calling distance.

"Over there," replied Ginny, nodding at a middle-aged woman, wearing a floral dress and carrying a large shoulder bag.

"She keeps looking in the bag," said Toby. "She's got something in there."

As he finished speaking, the woman put her hand in the bag and brought something out. The four animals tensed, waiting to see what she would do. The woman looked around and then, obviously feeling that no-one was looking, she dropped something on the ground and quickly moved away. Toby ran over to look at what she had dropped. He called to the others, "Quick, it's meat. It smells funny. I think it's been poisoned."

The three cats joined him and looked at the pieces of chopped meat lying on the grass. They could all tell that the meat didn't smell quite as it should. Jake thought quickly.

"Stay here, Toby, and stop any of the dogs eating it. Some will eat it too quickly to realise it's been poisoned." He turned to Sherpa and Ginny. "Come on, we've got to stay with her and stop any animals from eating the meat she drops." And the three cats disappeared in the same direction taken by the woman.

Toby, left alone, was suddenly aware of a large Alsatian, who had noticed what looked like meat on the floor, and moved towards it with the obvious intention of enjoying an unexpected snack. However, before the dog had a chance to touch the meat, the little Jack Russell stepped in.

"Leave it!" snapped Toby, moving between the meat and the Alsatian. The big dog looked at Toby, surprised at being ordered about by such a small dog and feeling more than a little put out. He stared fiercely at the little upstart in front of him and growled intimidatingly.

"What?" he barked but Toby, not at all intimidated, stood his ground.

"Leave it," he said, firmly. "It's poisoned. The woman who's been vandalising the showground is putting down poisoned meat. Go back and tell all the dogs not to eat any meat they find on the grass."

He was so agitated that the Alsatian immediately believed him. He turned and went quickly back to the show ring and soon the air was filled with the sound of barking dogs, all passing on the message.

While Toby was dealing with the Alsatian, Jake and the others were nearing the woman, who was pretending to be absorbed in watching the dog agility class going on. Several more members of Spy Club approached, including Brian and Wesley. Jake quickly explained what was going on and said, "We've got to stop animals eating what she puts down."

Wesley frowned. "But it will still be there. How can we keep watch all the time? It needs removing but how can we let the humans know what's wrong with it?"

Suddenly Ginny hissed, "She's got her hand in her bag. She's going to drop some more."

Before Jake could tell one of the cats to guard the meat the woman was about to drop, Brian said, "Leave it to me."

He raced forward and when he reached the woman, before she had a chance to remove her hand from her bag, he leapt up and took hold of the bag in his teeth. Taken completely by surprise, the woman yelled and pulled her empty hand out of the bag. She hung on tightly to the bag, but Brian was determined to get it off her and she and Brian started a tug of war over the bag.

By now nearly all the members of Spy Club had arrived and watched anxiously as some members of the public, unaware of what the woman had been doing, tried to help her. The cats milled around, getting in everyone's way, trying to keep the humans from getting close to the struggling dog and woman. Toby appeared and joined in, snapping at people's heels. Not wanting to be left out, he'd asked the Alsatian to guard the meat.

Suddenly Brian pulled the handbag off the woman's shoulder and onto the floor. The woman looked around quickly and then took to her heels across the showground. She appeared to be heading towards the car park. The onlookers who had been trying to help her stood watching her go, looking undecided, not sure now what was going on.

Her progress towards the car park was hampered by the fact that the showground was so busy, and she hadn't gone far when a black and white streak, appearing out of nowhere, raced after her. As he reached her, Tarran leapt into the air, crashing onto her back in a tackle the England rugby team would have been proud of! She hit the ground hard and rolled over. Before she knew what was happening the woman was lying on her back on the grass, staring up into the dog's snarling face. When she tried to struggle away, he showed her a set of very sharp, very efficient looking teeth and she realised it would be wiser to stay completely still.

"Oh, well done, Tarran," shouted Jake.

By now Ma, Pa and Claire had turned up, someone having rushed to tell Claire that her dog was attacking a member of the public!

Pa looked around at all the cats and dogs and knew that something important was going on. He turned to the Colonel, who had been running the agility class and had come to sort out the confusion, and said, "Something odd is going on. Brian wouldn't just attack someone. I think we should hang on to that woman for the moment."

People were muttering and the words 'savage' and 'uncontrolled' were being mentioned by members of the crowd and the Colonel, not having Pa's newly gained understanding of what the animals were doing, was looking a little undecided.

He had a great respect for Pa, but it wouldn't do the reputation of the show any good to have people saying that savage dogs were allowed to run free and attack people for no reason.

Pa had no such concerns. He looked back at Brian, still determinedly holding the woman's bag in his mouth. He turned to his daughter and said, "Claire, go and look in the bag."

Claire did as her father asked, Brian giving up the bag to her immediately. She looked inside and found a plastic bag full of chopped up pieces of stewing steak. She looked at Pa in confusion. "It's just meat. Surely Brian wouldn't attack her to get the meat! He's not an aggressive dog."

People around her were starting to mutter comments about Brian's 'vicious' attack and Claire's eyes filled with tears. Ma went over to her and put her arms around her shoulders. She looked closely at the meat and then bent down to sniff it.

"It smells off to me," she said, loudly enough for all those standing near them to hear. "I'll lay odds it's poisoned."

A babble of noise started as people, hearing Ma's comment, began to speculate about what was going on. Like a game of Chinese Whispers, Ma's comment spread around the people close by, inevitably getting changed until one poor woman was told that the woman lying on the grass had been poisoned!

The Colonel, having heard what Ma had said, finally decided that Pa was right. They should hang on to the woman until things were made clear. The Colonel thought very highly of both Ma and Pa, and he thought Ma was a wonderful woman. If Ma said the meat in the woman's bag was poisoned that was good enough for him.

Pa and the Colonel walked over to where Tarran was guarding the woman, growling whenever she attempted to get up.

Before they could say anything, Mad Mary appeared, worried that her dog had disgraced himself. As she saw Tarran pinning the woman to the ground her heart sank. Then she looked more closely at the woman lying on the floor and took a deep breath.

"Hallo, Maggie," she said. "Up to no good again?"

Pa and the Colonel turned to Mad Mary. "You know her?" asked Pa.

"Oh yes," she replied. "She's Old Joe's stepdaughter and a nasty piece of work, just like her daughter."

"Her daughter?" echoed the Colonel.

"Yes. Her daughter, Melanie, is one of the two thieves who were caught breaking into the village houses a few weeks ago." Mad Mary looked with disgust at the woman glaring at her. "I don't think we have to look any further for our vandal, do you?"

She made no attempt to move Tarran away from his prisoner. In fact, she looked at him with growing pride, relishing the fact that her 'unruly' dog had been the one to catch the vandal and was making quite sure she didn't escape.

By now a huge crowd had gathered round them, all talking nineteen to the dozen in very loud voices and making a terrific din. Pa held up his hand and it said a lot about the respect he was held in by the villagers, that the din instantly stopped and anyone still speaking did so in a very quiet voice.

Claire, Ma and the animals had also made their way over, Ma firmly holding Maggie's bag. Seeing Ma with her bag, Maggie gave her a venomous look. She knew that the contents of the bag would support Mad Mary's comment about her being the vandal. She'd have a hard time explaining why she was walking round the showground with a bag full of poisoned meat. Not being an animal lover, she hadn't cared that she would, at the very least, make some dogs extremely ill.

"I think we'd better take this lady to the tea tent and find the police," said Pa. "I'm surprised they haven't been attracted by all the noise. After all, they are supposed to be keeping an eye on things!"

CHAPTER THIRTEEN

The Colonel and Pa lifted Maggie from the ground and escorted her towards the tea tent. She tried to struggle but they were closely followed by Tarran and Brian who, both determined not to let her escape, growled in stereo every time she tried to pull away. Eventually, she realised that it would be in her best interests not to annoy the dogs, who both looked ready and happy to tear her to bits.

The rest of Spy Club followed behind them, attracting quite a lot of interest from the show visitors, intrigued by the collection of cats and dogs. The visitors also tried to follow but Pa firmly asked them to go back to enjoying themselves, which they reluctantly did. His apparently casual comment that the animals had gathered round them because they smelt the meat, was realistic enough to dispel everyone's interest in the gang of animals, which had been his intention.

Toby wanted desperately to go with the other club members, but remembered the poisoned meat, still lying on the floor. He looked across to where the Alsatian was still on guard and watched with relief as the dog's owner carefully picked up the meat in some paper. He had heard Ma's comment about it probably being poisoned. Knowing that it was the only meat the woman had managed to put down, Toby was able to run after the fast-disappearing group of animals and humans with a clear conscience.

One of the committee members was sent to find the two policemen, who were discovered looking round one of the craft tents. Uncomfortably aware that they hadn't exactly been doing their job, (being convinced, unlike Jake, that the vandal only acted at night) they hurried to the tea tent where they found Ma, Pa, Mad Mary and the Colonel standing beside a very bad-tempered looking woman, who was sitting on one of the chairs surrounded by what looked like a guard of cats and dogs.

"Right," said Sergeant Brown, attempting to take control of the situation. He had been rather embarrassed not to be found patrolling the showground but rather looking in the craft tents for his wife's birthday present! "Firstly, let's get these animals out of here."

"They stay!" said Pa firmly, to the surprise of Ma and the others and especially Sergeant Brown. "They were involved in the capture of this woman, whom I believe to be the person who has been vandalising the showground. We need to keep an eye on them in case it's upset them."

Pa avoided looking at the amazed expression on Ma's face, knowing he would have to think up an acceptable explanation for his strange comment before they were alone.

Not being willing to take Pa on about whether the animals stayed or not, Sergeant Brown decided to forget them and concentrate on the important thing.

"On what grounds do you make that accusation?" he asked. "What makes you think she has anything to do with the vandalism?"

"Look in her bag," responded Pa.

The sergeant looked at the other policeman. "Watkins, examine the bag."

PC Watkins opened the bag and found the plastic bag of meat. He looked at the sergeant with a puzzled expression.

The sergeant looked at Pa and raised his eyebrows as if to say, "So what!"

"It's poisoned!" said Ma bluntly.

At that moment the Alsatian and his owner appeared in the tea tent. The man handed the paper containing the poisoned meat to the sergeant, who handed it hurriedly to PC Watkins.

"I found it in the grass outside the show ring," said the man "I gather that it may be poisoned. It's lucky none of the dogs ate it." He nodded to Pa and the others and left with his dog.

"Thanks a lot!" shouted Toby to the Alsatian, who barked back, "Any time." As he followed his owner he was already imagining the tale he would tell to the neighbouring cats and dogs back home!

He followed his owner out of the tent and Toby went to join Brian and Tarran on guard. Jake and the cats settled in their usual place in the tea tent to watch what would happen next. They saw Ma looking at them with a very puzzled expression on her face. She recognised most of the cats but couldn't understand what they were all doing there.

Pa saw her looking and quickly drew her attention away from them and back to the discussion going on with the humans. He was explaining to the two policemen how they had come to realise that Maggie was the vandal and he asked Ma to explain her part in it all. She was happy enough to do that and it successfully kept her from wondering about the animals.

The cats talked quietly amongst themselves, well satisfied with the results of Spy Club's second mission, and relieved that they didn't have to try to explain things to the humans now.

"How many other members of that family are there?" said Sherpa jokingly. "Maybe they should just lock them all up. Save everyone a lot of trouble."

The cats smiled but all of them couldn't help feeling Sherpa had a good point.

Jake looked round proudly at the members of 'his' club. "Well, boys and girls, we did it again. You really are a brilliant team."

The cats all looked round at each other with great satisfaction.

"Not bad, I suppose," said Max in an unimpressed tone of voice. He looked round at a sea of disappointed faces. Then he grinned, something they rarely saw Max doing, and added, "It's the first time I've seen you all in action and Jake's right – you are a brilliant team."

The disappointed looks gave way to smiles of satisfaction. Max's praise was something not easily given and all the more precious for that reason.

Then their attention was drawn back to the group of humans. Maggie had said nothing but, after hearing what Pa and the others had to say, the police felt convinced that they had their culprit and Sergeant Brown was in the process of arresting Maggie and handcuffing her.

As they left to take her to the police station in Littlebury, the sergeant told Pa and the others that they would all be needed to give statements, along with any of the show's visitors who had witnessed the scene by the show ring. Pa promised they would collect as many names and addresses as they could, to make the police's job easier.

Then Ma, predictably, said, "Come on, let's have a nice cup of tea." As she went across to the urn, the vicar appeared in the doorway, looking rather alarmed.

"Someone said my cat was here. They said he's been arrested!" She obviously didn't think that this was beyond the bounds of possibility and looked across to where Beelzebub was sitting amongst a crowd of cats and dogs.

"What have you been up to now, Bee?" she asked him severely. Beelzebub had been a notoriously badly behaved kitten and Sally thought it quite believable that he had somehow got himself arrested, in spite of the innocent, 'butter wouldn't melt in my mouth' look he was giving her. He got up and went over to her, rubbing round her legs, and she bent down to stroke him, smiling and easily won over by his wheedling.

Ma, busy with the tea, watched Sally and her cat and said, "You missed all the excitement. We've caught the vandal. Come and sit down and have a cup of tea and we'll tell you all about it."

Sally, with a quick, slightly puzzled look at Beelzebub, back with the crowd of cats and dogs, went over to join the humans and tried her best to follow the rambled tale that Ma, Mad Mary and Claire were all telling her at the same time.

Pa, leaving them to it, got some cat treats and took them over to the group of animals. He looked at them and they looked at him. He had absolutely no doubt now that these animals were working together, working very efficiently together, and knew exactly what they were doing and what was going on.

"Good job, gang," he said quietly, and he put down treats for all the animals. Jake got up and rubbed against Pa's leg. He bent down to stroke the cat.

"So you're the leader, are you? I'll remember that."

He left the cats and went to get some treats for the three dogs. Brian and Tarran were being treated as heroes for catching Maggie, but they both knew it was a team effort. However, for Tarran, it was a change to have the humans praising him instead of yelling at him to behave and he was thoroughly enjoying it.

Brian looked across at the cats, all happily munching away, and caught Wesley's eye. Wesley smiled at him and Brian smiled back and nodded.

Pa and the Colonel went to the secretary's tent to put out a carefully worded message, asking for witnesses to the earlier 'incident' by the dog rings to leave their names and addresses with the secretary. Jenny then found herself not only taking down the information but discussing, over and over again with excited visitors, the events of the afternoon. By the time she had finished taking down the names and addresses of all the people who said they were witnesses, she was heartily sick of the whole story.

After eating his share of the treats, Mangy Tom got up and said he must be off. Sooty and Patch said they'd go with him. Jake thanked them for all their help. Sooty grinned. "Since meeting you and your mates, life hasn't been at all dull, I have to say." And the three cats disappeared out through the entrance flap, round the back of the tent and into the undergrowth.

Then Sherpa turned to Beelzebub. "Do you think I'll be able to get a lift with the vicar again? All this toing and froing isn't doing my paws any good!"

"How about me?" added Leo.

Beelzebub grinned. "She's getting used to being the local cat taxi."

Just then Mrs Whittacker appeared at the entrance. "Is my dog in here?" she asked. "What's he been up to?"

Within seconds she was sitting down, with a cup of tea in front of her, and the tale of Maggie's capture was being told yet again.

"I'm glad we caught the vandal and the show can go ahead without any more problems," said Wesley, "but, in a way, I'm sorry it's over. It's been very exciting." He saw them all looking at him. "Well, okay, it wasn't very nice sometimes."

"Don't worry Wesley," said Libby. "No doubt Jake will find something else for us to investigate before too long."

Jake looked put out. "I don't invent things," he said defensively.

Libby grinned. "No, but you love it when they happen."

All the cats laughed and Jake was forced to join in. There was an element of truth in what both Wesley and Libby had said. In spite of moments of danger and unpleasantness, Jake enjoyed the thrill of the chase.

By now visitors to the show were beginning to drift off home, full of the exciting events they had witnessed or been told about. The vicar had gone home with her own cat and two passengers, highly amused at the way Sherpa and Leo had made it plain that they wanted a lift. Fortunately, she was a woman who accepted things very easily and she didn't think to question their behaviour.

The workers and stall holders started putting things away and eventually the showground emptied and peace descended.

Ma and Pa debated whether to go home but decided to stay for the final night 'just in case'. Claire took Brian off home, feeling that he wasn't needed any more, and Mad Mary left with Max and Tarran, Tarran still basking in the praise for his capture of Maggie. He and Max were deep in conversation as they left and Jake and the others wondered what they were talking about.

Left alone at last, the four cats and Ma and Pa, after a quick check of the showground, settled down in the caravan for a good night's sleep, ready for the final day of the show – Bank Holiday Monday – always the busiest and most interesting day.

CHAPTER FOURTEEN

After an uninterrupted night, Monday morning dawned bright and sunny again. Pa got up early and made a tour of the showground, accompanied by the cats but, not unexpectedly, found nothing wrong. To his surprise though, he found Old Joe's battered van hidden behind the toilet block and remembered that they still hadn't found out what Joe was doing at the showground so late on Friday night.

When he got back to the caravan, he was clearly relieved to be able to tell Ma all was well. However, they spent the time over their breakfast discussing Old Joe's strange behaviour. They would simply *have* to find out what he had been up to!

As they were finishing breakfast, the sound of cars arriving told them that the stall holders and show workers were arriving to set up for the day. Ma got the tea urn going and Pa went out to check that no problems had cropped up.

Mad Mary, Claire and Simon arrived. Simon was looking forward to the day at the show but also the thought of a day away from his work was very appealing. He had been working very hard and felt that he deserved a day off.

They were accompanied by Brian, Max and Tarran. They were also accompanied by a tall bearded young man, who strode across to Ma, wrapped his arms around her in a bear hug and gave her a big kiss. Ma gazed dumbfounded at her son and gasped, "Peter! What are you doing here? I thought you were still in Australia."

Peter grinned at his mother. "Couldn't miss our village show now, could I? And, from what Claire's been telling me about vandals and fires and I don't know what else, it seems to me you need me to keep an eye on you all."

Ma gave him a gentle clip round the ear, but then gave him a hug of her own. She was absolutely delighted to have her big son back home again.

"When did you get home?" she asked.

"I got back from Australia yesterday," he answered. "I travelled back home last night, only to find the house locked, dark and totally empty. Claire and Simon put me up for the night and filled me in on what's been going on lately." He looked over to the side of the tent to where the animals had congregated in their usual place.

"I gather the animals have been getting involved too. I was obviously wrong to go travelling to find some excitement. I should have stayed home!"

Everyone laughed and the animals watched happily, knowing that Ma would be over the moon to have Peter back home for a while. They knew that she missed him a great deal although she never said anything. Pa, too, would be surprised and happy to see his son again.

Peter turned to the cats. "Hallo, you spoilt brats. How are you all?" He went over to the group of animals and gave the cats a fuss. They rubbed round him trying to show how pleased they were to see him. Then he turned to Max and Tarran. "Hallo Your Majesty," he said jokingly to Max. "How's the king today?"

Max looked down his nose at Peter but allowed him to stroke his head. He had a soft spot for the boy who had once not known that you shouldn't try to catch a cat by his tail! Then Peter turned to Tarran.

"Well, so this is the madcap dog Mad Mary's adopted. Seems to me that you redeemed yourself yesterday. Two brave dogs in the family." He fussed both the dogs and Tarran beamed at being referred to as one of the family.

Just at that moment Pa walked in and, going straight to Ma and Mad Mary at the urn, didn't see Peter kneeling with the animals. Ma put a severe look on her face and said, "I'm glad you've come, Pa. We've got a young tearaway causing trouble." She nodded over to where Peter and the animals were watching to see how he would react.

He turned, clearly ready to give the "young tearaway" a piece of his mind, but his jaw dropped when he saw his son sitting grinning at him. He went over to Peter, who stood up and gave his father a hug. The animals all beamed at them and Pa, looking down, saw the happy faces and winked at them. He felt a little sad that he couldn't tell his family, especially his son, what he had discovered about the cats and dogs, but he knew they would think he was mad and probably send for a straitjacket! There were times when he still wasn't a hundred percent sure himself that they wouldn't be right!

Meanwhile, typically, Ma had made them all cups of tea and they sat at a table together, listening to Peter's tales of his travels and telling him about the exciting events of the past couple of months.

Just before the show was due to open two policeman walked in, PC Watkins and another constable, PC Evans. They had been sent to patrol the showground, even though no-one expected any more incidents. Within seconds they were sitting at the table with Pa and the others, cups of tea in front of them, and the talk returning to the vandalism.

The animals listened carefully to what PC Watkins had to say. Apparently, Maggie had been charged with all sorts of things, including arson, damage to property and endangering life. At first, she had refused to say anything but, eventually, on the advice of a solicitor she had admitted everything, saying she had targeted the village show as an act of vengeance for her daughter's arrest. She blamed the villagers, but for some reason she also seemed to blame Old Joe, even though he had had nothing to do with Melanie's arrest. However, she had insisted that she had not realised that Joe was still in the tent when she set fire to it and the police believed her. The animals, too, were glad to think that it hadn't been a deliberate act.

Old Joe, now home from hospital and reunited with Bruiser, hadn't been surprised when told the identity of the vandal. According to Joe, Maggie had always been "the child from hell, who had grown up to be the woman from hell." He would never understand how his beloved wife had managed to produce such a horrible person. Like Bruiser, he felt that Melanie was exactly like her mother, unpleasant and a troublemaker.

The policeman talking to him and taking his statement, who had happened to be PC Watkins himself, had been more than a little taken aback at Old Joe's outspoken comments.

However, Joe was a little less forthcoming when asked why he was at the showground so late on Friday night. He had eventually admitted that he had gone to replace some of his entries because they were not his! Apparently, they had come from a greengrocer's in Littlebury, who had a reputation for excellent produce. Joe's conscience had pricked him and he went to get rid of the originals and put his own in their place.

He obviously felt ashamed of what he had done and rather unhappy at having to tell people about it. When PC Watkins asked why he had done it he mumbled something about being desperate "to beat James Tudsbury for once."

Both humans and animals laughed when PC Watkins told them this but then they all became more serious when they realised that his escapade had nearly ended very badly.

The animals had sat listening to all the discussion, silently congratulating themselves in being right in thinking Maggie was acting out of revenge.

Eventually the group of humans got up and went to get on with the jobs assigned to them. The police went to patrol the showground, although they obviously managed to find time to enjoy the show, as both went home with several items from the craft tents and PC Evans with a large teddy bear won on the hoopla stall. He was over the moon with this, knowing his wife, who had not been happy at him doing overtime on Bank Holiday Monday, would be totally forgiving at the sight of a beautiful, quite expensive looking bear for their young daughter, who would instantly love it.

Peter and Simon went to look round the attractions although both Ma and Claire knew that one of the biggest attractions would be the beer tent where the two men, who got on well together, would have a drink and catch up on each other's news. Mad Mary and Claire went to take their turn at the tombola stall and Ma continued to produce oceans of tea and coffee.

News of the previous day's events had travelled and people came from much further away than usual to visit the showground. Numbers were well up on previous years and Pa had to phone the farmer, William Lucas, who owned the two fields making up the showground, to ask if they could use another field for extra car parking. The farmer, who happened to be at the show with his family, was happy to agree. Takings for the Monday were almost double what they usually were. The stall holders sold out of nearly everything they had for sale and the food vendors were more than happy to have to send out for more supplies.

The cats and dogs, left to their own devices, wandered round the showground. Even Tarran was with them. For some reason it was assumed he was now responsible enough to be left off his lead, so he wandered happily round with the others, after a stern warning from Max to behave himself.

The vicar arrived with Beelzebub, Sherpa and Leo in tow. She complained that she felt like the Pied Piper except that she had cats following her not rats! The three newcomers joined Jake and the others and attracted a lot of attention, going around in such a big group. Especially when Mangy Tom and Toby arrived.

Mrs Whittacker had decided to come to the show again and had brought Toby with her. She usually only came on the Sunday but, being someone who loved a bit of gossip, she had come to discuss the previous day's events and, especially, her dog's part in them! Like Toby, she had enjoyed the bit of excitement it had brought to their otherwise uneventful lives.

After a little while the animals broke up into groups of two or three to continue their browse around the showground. The attention was becoming a little nerve wracking for Brian and particularly for Tarran, who got rather over excited and had to be spoken to severely by Max. They all arranged to meet later behind the tea tent by Ma and Pa`s caravan, to have a final chat before going their separate ways.

When they got there, they found Sooty and Patch waiting for them and Spy Club was more or less complete. Jake looked around at them all.

"Well, everyone, we've shown that last time wasn't a fluke. I'll say it again -we really are a brilliant team."

There were nods and murmurs of agreement from the rest of the animals. They all felt that the whole situation had ended very satisfactorily. Especially Brian! To his great relief, Claire had decided not to enter him in any of the dog show classes.

However, to everyone's amazement, Mad Mary had entered Tarran in one of the late afternoon obedience classes. The entry form, which the animals had seen Claire collecting from the secretary's tent, had been for Mad Mary not herself.

However, the amazement everyone, human and animal, had felt at Tarran being entered in an obedience class was nothing to the sheer astonishment and disbelief they had felt when he actually came third out of a class of ten! Mad Mary was absolutely bursting with pride and everyone else was bursting with shock.

"How did you manage it?" asked Jake wide eyed, when Tarran had come out of the show ring. "You hardly know the first thing about obedience."

Tarran looked a bit sheepish. "When we found out that Mad Mary had entered me, Max told me what the commands meant and went over the routine with me."

Max smiled grimly. "I had to do something. Mad Mary *would* enter him – why do you think everyone calls her Mad Mary? – and I couldn't let him show her up. I've seen enough obedience classes over the years to know how they go. It was quite easy."

That had been what Max and Tarran had been talking about as they had left the showground the previous day. They had just learnt what Mad Mary had done.

Max looked at Tarran with some satisfaction. "I have to say he is a quick learner and he didn't disgrace us."

Tarran looked at Max, surprised at the praise. Usually, if Max had anything to say about him, it was sarcastic.

"I couldn't have done it without Max's help," he said, wanting to say something nice to Max in return. Max's praise meant more to him than the yellow rosette, which Mad Mary was showing to everyone and anyone who would look at it.

Now, sitting behind the tea tent with the rest of the cats and dogs, it seemed as if Tarran had actually become a fully-fledged member of Spy Club. He finally felt accepted by them all and it was a good feeling, one he had never had before.

One more satisfying ending to the show was that Old Joe won first prize for his onions, knocking James Tudsbury into second place. The news and the red rosette, which Mad Mary took round to him after the show had finished, were a real tonic to Old Joe. He had apparently completely forgotten that he'd tried to cheat!

The animals discussed what the police had told them about Maggie's confession and Wesley, ever ready with a joking comment, said, "She'll be able to go into a cell next to her daughter!"

They all laughed. "Let's hope that's the end of the whole thing," said Libby anxiously, and the rest of the animals nodded in complete agreement.

Then Sherpa looked at Jake with a wicked grin on his face. "What have you got lined up for us next then?" he asked jokingly. "We need to have something exciting to keep us occupied." He gazed around at the others, who all looked half concerned and half hopeful. The events of the past couple of months had been both exciting and scary.

"Remember what you said to me a few days ago," Jake reminded him. "Be careful what you wish for."

The animals laughed and the atmosphere became relaxed and contented. Eventually, some of them got up, ready to leave. Beelzebub, Sherpa and Leo went off to find the vicar and get their lift home. Toby went to look for Mrs Whittacker, whom he eventually found in the tea tent still talking to Ma and getting all the little details she hadn't managed to get elsewhere. Sooty and Patch started to make their way home along with Mangy Tom, who had been invited to share their tea, their owner, Mr McMurty, being an animal lover who would feed any animals which turned up at his door!

Jake and the rest of his family's pets were finally left alone and made their way back inside the tea tent to find Ma and the others. The day was winding down and everyone seemed to think that, in spite of all the problems, it had been the best Summer Show they could remember. It was certainly one which wouldn't easily be forgotten by the villagers, especially the committee members, who all gave a sigh of relief that it had ended so successfully. Once the visitors had left they started the job of dismantling things, although most of the work would be done the following morning. Mixed with the sense of satisfaction, there was also a feeling of sadness that it was all over for another year.

Eventually Ma and Pa, along with Peter and the cats, made their way back home, to be followed shortly by Mad Mary, Claire and Simon, along with their animals. Peter's surprise return had given rise to a family get together, Ma and Pa suggesting they all had supper together at their house. As could be expected, Ma's food cupboards were always full, so a sudden demand to provide a meal for six people was no problem.

While the family eventually settled in the large sitting room, the animals, happy together but feeling tired, settled in the kitchen and talked quietly to one another.

At one point, Pa came into the kitchen to make a fresh pot of tea. While the kettle was boiling, he went over to speak to the animals.

"Well, you lot. Another good job done. You've got a good team there, young Jake."

He seemed to have completely lost any uncertainty about the animals and what they were doing and was quite unself-conscious talking to them.

The animals got up and crowded round him and he petted them all one at a time, talking to them as if they understood everything he was saying, which indeed they did. It was a bit of a one-sided conversation because, although they responded to his comments, he had not, as Max had suggested, had a crash course in talking or understanding cat and dog.

Eventually they were interrupted by Ma, coming into the kitchen to see what was holding up the tea. She looked indulgently at Pa, surrounded by cats and dogs, and said tolerantly, "What are you doing there, Pa? Anyone would think you were one of them." She laughed at her ridiculous suggestion and went over to finish making the tea.

But Pa looked at the animals and, as they looked back at him, he winked at them. Little did Ma know how close to the truth she had come.

ABOUT THE AUTHOR

I am a retired English teacher, living in a village on the Northamptonshire / Leicestershire border, with my husband and three cats. I have a daughter and son and three granddaughters. I have been cat mad all my life and have owned several Siamese cats over the years.

THE SPY CLUB BOOKS

Although all the humans and some of the animals in the Spy Club books are fictitious, some of them are based on real animals. The roots of the Spy Club stories go way back to 2000, when I got my seal point, Jake. Like Ma, in a very short space of time we had acquired Libby, Ginny and Wesley. They were all very spoilt and at one point my husband asked what they did to earn their living because he never saw them doing any work. I told him that was because they were spies and worked undercover. After that we would come up with more and more tales about their exploits. Jake was senior spy and Wesley was the trainee. Libby was Big L and Ginny, who had failed her spying exams, was the secretary with a pink laptop and pink mobile.

I always said that, when I retired, I would write a book about it all. However, in spite of retiring ten years ago, nothing happened until the first Lockdown when inspiration suddenly hit. Our four Siamese became the main characters, Max belonged to my sister and Sherpa to our neighbours. Toby is based on a friend's daughter's dog and, in looks and character, they are all exactly the same in the books as they were in real life. The other characters are all fictitious, as are the Valley Villages and surrounding area.

TARRAN

When I came to start writing "Spy Club Book Two – The Valley Villages Summer Show", I decided that I needed another dog character. There were numerous cats in Book One but only two dogs. Enter Tarran. Tarran is not a made-up character, he is my granddaughter's dog and, after talking to her about it, we decided he would be ideal as the newcomer. You will have to read the book to find out what the fictitious character is like, but the real Tarran is something of a personality. Izzy is training him to be a flyball dog and he recently won a "Best Improved" award. He is not a dog who will give his affection easily, but I seem to have become a favourite with him. Maybe because I told him I was going to make him famous! Hopefully, the character as portrayed in the book will become a favourite with readers.

Lightning Source UK Ltd.
Milton Keynes UK
UKHW011545170922
409025UK00001B/11